TEST RUN: IN HIS IMAGE

MARJAYE FREE

DEDICATION

This book is dedicated to all those who have been supportive and encouraging.

FOREWORD

I met Marjaye Free in a childcare class at a community college. We became team members on an assignment that required us to read each other's papers. As I read Marjaye's papers, her words were like picture frames of a movie, guiding me through emotions and events—alive in my senses. Her words are divinely inspired, while touching upon contrasts between religion and Christianity —between theology and practice. Travel along with her on this journey, *Test Run: In His Image* and enjoy the character of the Messiah.

--Linda Waters, MA, Marriage and Family Therapy

PROLOGUE

Three Years Earlier

Messiah opened his eyes and checked his watch; it was eight-forty. He stretched his arms forward and turned his head to look at the train's schedule; it was running on schedule. *Twenty minutes and I'll be able to take a long nap in comfort.*

He sat up, leaning his head on the vending machine, and ran his hands through his long, thick, wooly, black hair. He opened his Bible and began to read; then closed it, got up, and walked around, observing the number of homeless people lying on the ground. He stopped, and turned slowly, directing his attention to the men with briefcases and the women with big, expensive pocketbooks. Some of them strutted through the terminal with name-brand clothing from head to toe, jewelry sparkling from their hands, necks and wrists.

Their chins stuck up like their necks were bound in a brace;

their noses scrunched, like there was some ferocious stench in the air. He shook his head from side to side in shame for them. A handful looked down at the faces of despair, and only a few reached in their pockets to offer something that could help one.

He shook his head again, sighing as he walked over to the window to take a seat on the bench. Unlatching his sandals, he stopped and looked up. To his dismay he saw Sandy Moller, deaconess of Love of Christ Church in New Jersey looking at him with disgust in her eyes. *She almost lost her home last year when she was laid off, and her husband left her. I hope she remembers how blessed she was that her job called her back six months later.*

He shook his head again, as his eyes fell upon Samuel Avalon, a prominent bishop in Brooklyn. The glare was so piercing that Messiah squinted his eyes, reacting to the ache in his heart. He smiled at him, hoping to soften his glare, but he couldn't see beyond Messiah's ragged attire and worn sandals.

"Oh Father, Father, Father, Father, I thought that I'd never have to return before my appointed time. I thought, I—"

"Good Morning, Laaadies, and Gentlemen; Northeast Regional 1-8-3 Southbound to Washington, DC is now boarding at Track 18. Please gather your belongings and c'mon down," the jolly voice sang over the PA system.

Messiah stood up and walked down the stairs. To his delight, the line was not long, and there weren't many people on board. He saw Sally Moller again, her face tightened when she saw him boarding the same train as her. *I wonder if one of her church members became misfortuned would she still allow them to keep their titles?* Messiah thought, walking through the cars of the train to find a seat.

He found a seat in the front row of the second car facing the direction he would be traveling, and sat. The only bag he had contained a bag of chips, a bottle of water, and his passport.

"Oooh Lord, Father, I'm so tired of sleeping on those hard boxes. My goodness, they're so uncomfortable. And the newspapers really don't provide a lot of warmth. Hmm!"

"You know I'm not a complainer, but this body is just not me. *And* these people that I keep sacrificing for, most are not learning anything from the efforts I make. *But* for you I will do it and because of who I am, I know my efforts will not be in vain. There are still many people striving to do right." Messiah yawned. "I submit my will to you, Father.

"Sure wish I didn't have to come here as a homeless person. You know, I wouldn't have minded being a servant to the President, the First Lady and those two cute little girls. But homeless? That's what you came up with?"

"Dramatic effects, son!" His father's hearty voice laughed.

❧

"MESSIAH. MESSIAH," THE VOICE WHISPERED, "I'M SORRY, SON, that you must make this journey again, but there are too many souls crying for help, and thirsting for the Word. There are so many searching for guidance, teachings, love, freedom, deliverance, joy and peace.

"How long have we discussed something had to be done? The laborers have become *fewer* than few. The churches have become a money-making business for most of these preachers.

"Most of these ministers want a big church, with lots of people attending. Mega churches! That's what most of these guys are chasing, not souls. They're acting as if we don't know what we're doing. Can't they see if we gave them a small church, then they are where they're supposed to be for now?

"Everybody wants to be J.D. Drakes, but they don't want to do the work J.D. Drakes does. Where are the books? Where are their movies? What have they produced? What about seminars?

"If they initiated more time in being like *You* instead of J.D. Drakes, there'd be less hurt Christians running from the church. How come no one gets that, J.D. Drakes, Jason Bolsteen, Clayton Dollard and Joy Meyder are who they are because of us. They didn't make themselves. Their status is where we purposed them to be. How come they don't know this, yet they profess to be appointed shepherds?"

"Messiah, we need to give direction to some of these ministers and lost souls. We need to remind the strayed preachers what they were purposed to do. We need to encourage those ministers who aren't compromising the Word, or hurting our people so they're assured they aren't alone, and their efforts do not go unnoticed.

"There are broken families that need to be mended; there are misguided families that need to be set on the right track. There are families that are so trapped in bondage that the curse and strife are submerged deep down from one generation to the next.

"Minds are distorted, children are running around unwise; decent spouses are being bamboozled by conniving, manipulative spouses. Preachers are financially raping their members; they are destroying families, loved ones, marriages and the children of their own congregations.

"Messiah, you've seen it, they are even destroying their own homes; their children are out of control and they are using our name, to castrate their own flock.

"You know I like to let you handle business your own way; however, there are some people you will need to raise up spiritually, mentally, and emotionally. How you handle them is up to you and we will only communicate through prayers. Your earthly form is all you will have and Me through prayer.

"Believe me, Son, you've got your work cut out for you. As always, some will be easy to work with, some will be difficult, some will surrender and some will initiate their right to free-will. In the end, we will get the glory. Whatever the outcome, no one from this day forth will be able to say they didn't know.

"I'm almost embarrassed to bid you farewell after dropping this load on you, but I am confident that you will do a great job.

"I Love You, Son! Increase the Laborers, my Son. Increase the Laborers! Increase the Laborers!" The voice faded into oblivion.

❧ 1 ❧

BAD BLOOD

Tiffani sat in church with her eyes closed, meditating; the first of the year was two hours away. She looked forward to welcoming 2010. As she gave thanks for surviving the departing year, her mind ventured off to how mysterious a new year was: births, deaths, successes, downfalls; relationships: new ones, old ones and terminal ones, lay ahead unknowingly. She remembered her positive outlook for 2009; after all, the first black president was welcomed into office with his family. She was grateful to have witnessed his election.

But 2009 came through like a boulder wreaking havoc throughout the United States, and the world. The economy tore apart businesses, homes and families. Celebrities' deaths headlined the media continuously. The United States was body-slammed by crooked investors, bankers, businessmen, and the ramifications of poor political decisions made over the years.

She took a deep breath, concluding 2009 was probably the worst year she could remember because of the devastation that had come upon so many lives. It didn't just affect her, her friends and family, but the world, the rich, and the poor.

She squeezed her eyes tighter, rubbed her stomach and mumbled, "Thank You, Lord for my husband, my son, Kenya, and my babies. Thank You for protecting us this past year and please bless our family, the first family, this country and the world in 2010."

"You okay?" Kenya asked, elbowing her.

"Yeah, I was just reflecting and giving thanks, why?"

"You were groaning."

"And I told her you were getting your groove on," Marian chimed. Kenya elbowed Marian. There was always bad blood between Tiffani and Marian, making Kenya the buffer.

Kenya Florenton and Tiffani Bowen were best friends from the age of two. Living next door to each other, they became inseparable throughout childhood, building a strong defense through adolescence, battling Kenya's parents' ruthless, old-fashion ways, and Tiffani's parents' love for booze. They called each other every night, keeping one another informed of the drama in their homes.

It was no surprise that Kenya was the only one who knew Tiffani had left for Maryland to marry her high school sweetheart, Trevor Bowen the day of her eighteenth birthday party. Kenya appeared just as shocked as Tiffani's parents, friends and family when Tiffani did not show up.

Two years later, Kenya relocated and joined her friends to care for their first born, Trevor, Jr.

For three years, Kenya lived with Tiffani and Trevor, as their nanny and housekeeper. She took evening classes for media design. She saved her earnings, and eventually took a job at a local bank, purchasing her first townhouse. The townhouse had three bedrooms, an office and two and a half baths, and was located directly across the street from Tiffani.

Two years later, a pregnant Marian Lloyd moved eight houses from Kenya. Kenya baked a lemon cake, welcoming her into the neighborhood, and they exchanged phone numbers in case Marian needed help.

On a brisk night in September, Kenya drove Marian to the hospital, coaching her through the birth of her third daughter, Jacinta, forming a bond between the two that otherwise would not have existed.

⊗⊗

"KENYA, THIS IS MY LAST TIME GOING ANYWHERE WITH YOU and Marian," Tiffani snarled.

"Calm down, Tiff, I already got on her; we'll talk later," she whispered.

"No, Kenya. We won't discuss this later; I've had enough of Marian. She's your friend, not mine," Tiffani snarled, storming out the church.

"Don't worry about her, Kenya; she'll be a'ight," Marian assured.

"No, she won't, Marian! Why can't you just shut your mouth?"

"I'm telling you, it's the pregnancy. Those hormones got her acting crazy."

⊗⊗

"HEY BABE, HOW WAS SERVICE?" TREVOR ASKED, LOOKING AT his watch. "Was the preacher sick?"

"Uh-no, I just left early 'cause I'm tired," she whispered, wiping the tears from her eyes. "Is my prince asleep?"

"Sure is, you know I knows how to do the daddy thing. We played cops and robbers, and that memory game your son cheats on."

"Oh, *my* son?" Tiffani queried with a forced smile.

Trevor pulled her into his arms and rubbed her plumped belly; kissing her firmly on her lips. "What's wrong, babe?"

"Nothing."

"Hmmm, seems like nothin's got you home early, with salty lips, and a stiff back."

Trevor gently took her hand, and pulled her down on the sofa. "I'm gonna make us some tea, and then you gonna tell Daddy who been messin' with his girl."

Tiffani wiped the tears that rushed down her face when Trevor left the room. She thought about her situation with Kenya and Marian, wondering how this recent incident would affect her friendship with Kenya.

She told Trevor everything, and he listened without interruption. When she was finished, he wiped her face, and kissed it gently. "What do you think?" she asked.

"Uhmmm, I think you need to tell Kenya how you feel. You two have been friends too long; don't let something like this come between you."

"Kenya's just going to say the pregnancy's making me sensitive," Tiffani retorted.

"Now you know Kenya isn't like that. She's your sister; talk to her."

2

AGAPE LOVE

"**M**ommy, come here," little Trevor yelled from his bedroom. Trevor leaped out the bed, and raced to his son's room, putting on his robe. "Ssshhhhh," he whispered, "the queen's asleep."

Trevor leaped into his father's arms. "I'm hungry, I need pancakes," he sang, wrapping his arms around his father's neck.

"Lil Man, you need toothpaste. Where's my hello, my handsome daddy? Instead you're just thinking about pancakes," his father teased, tickling him.

"Hello, my daddy 'cause I'm hungry." Trevor giggled.

"Come on, let's brush our teeth, and make some breakfast."

"Yea, let's get Mommy!"

"Mommy's tired. Let's make a pancake surprise for her, okay?"

Trevor stood him on top of the vanity, washed his face and then took him downstairs to the kitchen. He opened the freezer to take out the frozen pancakes. "Daddy, I dun't want that pancakes."

"You don't? What other kind is there... I mean, do you want?"

"In the closet," his son said, pointing to the cabinet above the counter.

"Trev, Daddy may not do such a good job making these pancakes." He laughed. He reached for the box and turned it over and surprisingly he found a recipe on the back. "Look Trev-J, I think we might be in business."

"Yeaaaaaah." Trev-J screamed, jumping up and down.

"Now, if I were your mommy, I'd make these pancakes in what kind of bowl?" Trev-J shrugged his shoulder. "A big bowl?"

"Big bowl it is." Trevor looked under the sink, finding pots and pans. He sheepishly turned and looked over at his son and grinned. "Not there!"

"Not dere," Trev-J parroted.

He walked over to the cabinet next to the stove and was about to open it, when the doorbell rang. "Who's that?" Trevor asked, picking up his son.

"I dun know."

"Let's go see." They snuck into the living room, peeped through the drapes, spotted Kenya and waved.

"Big-T, will you open the door." Trevor shut the drapes, and then slowly reopened them; little Trev-J squealed, "It's Auntie Gia." He always called her by the short form of her middle name, Giandra. Trevor spun him around, and ran to the door.

"Hey, sis." Trevor laughed. "Happy New Year!"

"Same to you," she said, playfully punching him in his arm. "You do know it's cold outside, right?" She laughed.

"We're undercover," Trevor said.

"Yeah, we unercover," Trev-J repeated. Kenya reached out her arms, catching the leaping child.

"You unercover," she mimicked, kissing him. "Happy New Year's, Trev-J."

"We making pancakes," Trev-J announced. He grabbed her hand, pulling her into the kitchen.

"You're cooking?" Kenya looked at Trevor with a fake look of concern.

"Girl, go on. You ain't tasted nothin' till ya have pancakes at "Trev's Father & Son. Have a seat. We gonna knock you off your feet."

"I believe that." Kenya laughed.

She pulled out a chair and sat. Trevor climbed up in her lap, and placed his hands on both sides of her face. "Daddy looking for some bowl."

"God help us. You're a chef without a bowl?"

"Kenya, stop doubting perfection, and Trev-J, stop telling our secrets."

Kenya hugged Trev-J, stood and lifted him from her lap and settled him on a nearby chair. She walked to the lazy susan cabinet, pulled out the bowl and handed it to Trevor, shaking her head.

"Thank you, assistant." Trevor smiled. When she turned to walk back to her seat, Trevor grabbed her arm. "You two are fine, you know? It's just a disagreement." Kenya's eyes immediately spit the water they had been holding since she started her journey across the street.

"I don't know what happened; I would never do anything to hurt T—"

"Shhh, let me take Trev-J to the family room."

"Lil' Man, you wanna watch *Bible Man* while Daddy makes the pancakes?"

"Yea!" he shouted, jumping off the chair into his father's arms;

spreading his arms out. His father spun him around, walking out the kitchen.

Kenya shook her head between sniffles, and chuckled at their antics. Trevor was one of the good ones. She loved the bond he'd built with his son.

She also loved how he loved Tiffani. She admired his friendship, not only with his wife, but with her. He considered her his sister just as she considered him her brother. He was loyal to his family, he was also non-judgmental, making him easy to talk to.

"You ready for your first lesson, girl?" He pulled her out the chair and wrapped his arms around her. "Gian, you two are fine."

"I think she thinks I chose Marian over her, and that's not true. I was just trying to make peace."

Trevor grabbed a paper towel, and wiped Kenya's face, then looked down at his robe. "Girl, you got slob all over my robe." Kenya smiled, pushing him.

"Gian, you can only have peace if everyone involved wants peace. Peace isn't guaranteed just because people come together or befriend one another. Each of us has an agenda, good or bad."

"Marian's a raw person. She says whatever comes to her mind. I'm trying to teach her to think before she talks."

"Marian's an adult. What you're teaching her she already knows. She's just never suffered any consequences for her behavior. If Tiffani were to reciprocate her with her own treatment, she would have a problem with that."

"I just feel sorry for her. She has no family, no friends, just me."

"Is that the only reason you're friends with her?" Kenya stared out the kitchen window. She had no idea why she was friends with Marian. The tears rolled down her face.

"Gi?" Trevor called her name gently.

"Trev, I just feel like I need to help her so she and those kids won't be alone."

"Look sis, that's fine if you're comfortable doing that, but then you're going to have to accept the fact that she and Tiffani don't click. I don't want you thinking I'm putting this all on you, either; I'm not. Tiffani should've told you she had problems with this chick way before last night. You two are too tight to let stuff fester. I hate seeing either of you hurting and slobbering." He smiled.

"Trev, I don't know what to do... suppose she won't talk to me. She was really pissed last night. I should've followed her, but people started looking at me when Tiff stormed out. I didn't know what to do."

"I'll tell you what, let's get breakfast together, then we'll figure something out. Why don't you get the ingredients together, and I'll fix the coffee," Trevor said.

Kenya wiped her face, shooting him a suspicious look. "So, I'm making breakfast?"

"Naw, you're just getting the ingredients, and measuring. I'll help you stir." They both laughed.

Although Kenya still had no clue what events would take place when she faced Tiffani, she felt better after talking with Trevor. "I'm gonna check on Trev-J," she said.

When she returned, Trevor was leaning against the refrigerator reading the back of the pancake box. "I admire your intentions," she said, grabbing the box. "Let me help you before we end up hospitalized." She laughed.

She melted the butter, added milk and vanilla flavoring in a measuring cup. "Hey, this box don't say nothin' about vanilla flavoring," Trevor interrupted.

"You wanna make these pancakes *alone*?"

"Uh, no, thank you." Trevor leaned on the sink, watching her work. "Gian, you ever put two strange dogs in a room together?"

Kenya looked at him confused. "Two strange dogs? No, why would I do that? They'd kill each other," she answered innocently.

"Yep, but that's what you did when you tried to put Marian and Tiffani together in your little circle." He laughed.

Kenya stopped stirring and looked at him smiling at her. She picked up the dish towel, threw it at him, and began stirring again.

"I sure did, didn't I?" She laughed.

❦

"Happy New Year's, Mama!" Trevor said, embracing his wife.

"Happy New Year's." Kenya stood, picked Trev-J up, and carried him to his mother so they both could kiss her.

"Happy New Year, Kenya," Tiffani responded coldly.

Trevor looked at his wife, and then at Kenya. "Have a seat," he said, pulling out her chair.

"I'm fine," Tiffani said, walking over to make her coffee.

"Sit down. I'll get that for you, hon," Trevor said, pouring the cup of decaf, adding cream the way she enjoyed it. He then walked out the kitchen to the coat closet, grabbing his wool coat. He put it on, wrapped his scarf around his mouth, slipped on his gloves, walked back into the kitchen and sat down. "Can someone pass the pancakes?" he asked.

When Tiffani turned to pass him the pancakes, he was holding out his plate with all his outer-garments on and his mouth covered. "You are sooooo *stupid*." She stifled her laugh, trying to maintain her attitude. Kenya looked up from her plate and shook her head.

"How do I look?"

"I already told you," Tiffani answered.

"That's how you two look to me. This kitchen feels like an icebox and I've lost my appetite."

He put his plate down, looking first at his wife, and then at Kenya. "Ladies, today's the first day of 2010; we all know this isn't the way to start. You have been friends too long to allow Marian to come between you. I know both of you feel this is a real serious situation, but it's not. If, God forbid, something happened to either of you, the other would be devastated. I can't tell you all what to do, but I can say this: It pains me to see you two hurting. *Talk to each other!*"

"I didn't do anything to hurt Kenya," Tiffani retaliated, tears rushing down her face, "so why are you picking her side, Trevor?"

"Babe, I'm not taking anyone's si—"

"You're my husb—" Trevor placed his hand over his wife's hand, interrupting her.

"Trev-J, you finished?" he asked, noticing his son had cued in on their conversation.

"Yep, it's all gone."

"Let's wash our hands and I'll put on another B—"

"*Bible Man*," Trev-J finalized.

"You got it, buddy!" He swooped his son up, and walked out. When he returned, Tiffani and Kenya were playing with the rims of their coffee mugs.

"Anyone want more coffee?"

"I do," Kenya replied.

He replenished both his and Kenya's mugs, and returned to his seat. He took a long sip, then placed it down in front of him.

"Tiffy, you know you're the love of my life and I'd do anything for you. But you know I've always been honest with you, so, I

17

can't pick your side simply because you're my wife. That would take away from who I am, and disrespect the bond between you and Gia."

"You've had a problem with Marian since the first day you met; yet, you never told Gia. This woman has even said things to you when Gia wasn't around; but you never told her. Honey, you let it build up until you exploded."

"And Gia, like I explained to you earlier, Marian's just *your* friend. The one thing I'm sure about is Marian's butt got my two partners fighting and I ain't feeling no love up in here. Seriously ladies, I know you all aren't going to allow this woman to redefine the nature of your relationship."

"What do you mean 'redefine'?" Kenya asked, annoyed that he was implying Marian was controlling them.

"You and Tiffy have loved each other through the test of time; you all survived your parents' craziness; standing together through good and bad times. You've survived through the crap of other so-called friends trying to destroy your bond. Most importantly, you've loved each other through our relationship. Don't think I wanted you around when we first started dating; you two were inseparable. Ya made me sick..."

"*Trevor!*" Tiffany scolded, slapping his hand gently.

"I didn't know that," Kenya said.

"Girl please, you were my personal cock-blocker."

"*Trevor Bowen*, stop it!"

"Oh, now you want to defend her, huh? That's my girl; agape love's kicking in."

"Agape love?" Tiffani questioned.

"Yeah, baaaaaaaaabe, that love that passes all misunderstandings; you know, that *Jesus* Love, ladies. Now come on, talk this out and don't let another hour go by with this nonsense."

"My job here's done, I'm gonna go watch *Bible Man*," he said, imitating Trev-J, "and leave you guys; pull each other's hair, throw pots, do whatever it takes to get 2010 started right. I've been playing with a three year old, since yesterday."

He stopped and turned around. "Tiffani, speak what's on your heart, and Gia, let dem strange dogs out."

❧

KENYA MOVED TO TREVOR'S SEAT. "TIFFY, I'M SOOOOOO sorry." The tears rolled down her face and she put her hand on top of Tiffani's. "I never meant to hurt you. I was trying to help Marian feel accepted, to give her the kind of friendship we have."

Tiffani didn't speak. She bawled, her head down on the table, then she pulled Kenya's hand into hers. "I don't know what happened last night. Somethin' just got hold of me and made me strike out at you. It's just... Marian's always around us. She's not a nice person either. She's demeaning, insulting—"

"I know, she—" Kenya began.

"You know?" Tiffani inquired, lifting her head to look at Kenya. "Then why do you hang with her? Why do you want her around?"

"I don't know," Kenya interrupted her.

Tiffani pulled her hands from Kenya's and sat up. "Gian, you mean to tell me you know that this girl's a jerk, and you still keep bringing her around? Why?"

"Crazy, but I really don't know. I felt if she hung with us, she'd eventually stop being so hurtful to people because she'd learn what true friendship is. I'm just sorry it jeopardized our friendship."

"Kenya, no one can jeopardize our friendship unless we let

them. I mean, I think we can get through anything; even though I wanted to kick your butt last night. You know, uh... I thought she was becoming your best friend... replacing me," Tiffani sheepishly admitted.

"Are you crazy?" Kenya responded. "No one can come between us; *No One*. If our insane parents couldn't come between us, no one ever will. Our friendship was blessed by God when we were little girls, and what God puts together can't nobody tear it apart." They both laughed.

"You'd think I'd know that but this girl tries to come between us, and that's scary."

"Tiff, if that's what Marian was trying to do, she wasn't successful. I've been spending a lot of time with Marian to help her with her girls. I thought it'd be a good distraction for me, so that you and Trevor wouldn't always have a third wheel around you."

"Do you feel like a third wheel? We're family, Kenya; you're my sister."

"I'm twenty-six, no man, no children, and always hanging at your house. I eat mostly all my meals here," Kenya explained, pulling Tiffani's hand towards her again.

"Who cares. Would you throw me out if you were married?"

"Only if I couldn't get none." Kenya smiled.

"Well, obviously that ain't happening here," Tiffani teased, rubbing her belly.

"I'm sorry, Kenya," Tiffani said.

"Me too."

They both stood up, and hugged as the babies began kicking. "Ow! I got kicked," Kenya said, rubbing Tiffani's stomach.

"I wanna get kicked too," Trevor whined, racing to them to pull both of them into his arms, kissing their foreheads.

"Happy New Year, ladies! I'm proud of you. Now can we get out of this house?"

"Where are we going?" Tiffani asked.

"Let's go visit our families in New York for a few days."

"*New York?*" Tiffani and Kenya shouted.

"What happened to a peaceful New Year's?" Tiffani asked.

"That's a-g-a-p-e l-o-v-e, girls." Trevor spelled the word slowly, then he said it again, enunciating each syllable. "A *ga p e* love." Trevor laughed.

3

CHOSE YE THIS DAY

Adyson Haze Clark lay on the top bunk, searching the ceiling for some direction. Four more hours and he'd be leaving prison. "I ain't never coming back here," he whispered. He shifted his eyes from the ceiling to the wall, fighting the tears. "Three-and-a-half years. That's one-thousand-two-hundred annnd seventy-five days." He shifted his weight to his side to change the direction of his thoughts.

His anger rose when he thought about his mother. *What kind of mother doesn't visit her own son in jail?* "All that heifer cares about is that precious husband of hers." The anger fiercely stirred in him so he turned on his back.

"Yo Clark," called Dorsey Sparke, his cell mate. "You plan on us getting sleep tonight?"

Adyson lifted up on his elbow. "Man, just got things on my mind. Sparky, one mo' day's all I got, then I'm out of here."

"Then just go to sleep!"

Adyson lay back down. *Dorsey's such a punk. He's just pissed that I didn't follow him with that Jesus stuff.*

Dorsey and Brian Harris, now known as Wadi, his Muslim name, both prepared compelling arguments on who was the better God. Both being good friends of his, they had become bitter enemies as each tried to build their ministry in prison for a life with hopes for a better future.

Wadi had many followers for over three years, Dorsey included. Dorsey stopped attending meetings shortly after writing his mother and telling her about his Muslim classes. A week later, she sent him the King James Bible. He began reading it to compare the teachings; shortly after, he was trying to share that Bible with anyone who would listen.

Adyson enjoyed the Muslim teachings; he had learned a lot about being a strong, black man. He had never been a man of his word and he'd never taken responsibility for anything.

Prior to the classes, he never gave a thought about what he would do once he left the correctional facility. Now he was reading books, concerned about what he should do with his life after incarceration. The other thing about the Muslim teaching was that women stayed in their place; they had no rights and were submissive to man.

Dorsey's teaching was totally different. All men, meaning women too, were created in God's image. *How could that be when women were weak in mind, strength, and they were limited? Always crying and whining about something. Why can't I go to sleep?* The sweat rolled down his forehead as he turned over again. He focused back on Dorsey. *Why'd that fool start acting crappy with me because we had different beliefs?*

That's why Wadi can't stand Christians; he says they always think they know everything and never wanna listen to what anyone else gotta say.

Then they wanna judge. Adyson was agitated with Dorsey; he embarrassed him in front of the other cell mates when he called himself predicting that without Jesus, Adyson would return to prison. *Like some white man would ever save my black butt.*

He flipped over in his cot, hoping to annoy Dorsey. *He betta not say one freakin' thang to me. I was dumb enough to promise him I'd visit his wife and family to see how they're doing. I ain't visiting no one, punk! Hmmph, and what about that Adonyjah? He visited me one time in three years. He wouldn't even answer my calls last week, or come pick me up today. I guess dem so-called letters he call himself sending me for encourage-ment and that chump change, was his idea of support.*

Where in da world am I gonna stay? They all wanna act like they're better than me. I wish Aryngton had his own place; I could crash with him.

ZaBryna told him his room was prepared but in his heart, he knew that there were just too many people in that house; plus, his father didn't want him there. "Well he's in a wheelchair now, so he's got no vote in this," he said out loud. He rolled over and could see the light coming through the small barred window. He was glad daylight was entering his cell; now his mind could rest.

"Adyson," Dorsey said, "we need to talk."

"Naw, I'm straight."

"So, we just gonna part like dis?"

"Wadi, my brotha," Adyson greeted, ignoring Dorsey. "It's been good, man; thanks for teaching me the way, man." He shifted his eyes toward Dorsey to see if he was listening.

"It's what I do," responded Wadi. "Don't let dem get you twisted about who's the savior of the black race, man. Stand up, be a man, attend the mosque, read so you can grow and teach others. Keep in touch too." Adyson shook his hand and met the guards to go through the doors.

"Adyson, God bless, man," Dorsey yelled. "I want you to have this." He extended his hand to give him the Bible his mother sent him.

"Man, I can't take your Bible! I ain't got time to read this. I got the Quran, and besides, I gotta get a job," Adyson argued.

Dorsey pushed the book into his hand. "I know you don't, but I still want you to have it, man. I wrote some scriptures I'd like you to read. The first and most important is John 3:16, then read 2 Corinthians 5:17 and Romans 6:3-5. Then," he said with excitement, "you can compare it to the Quran."

"Man, Sparky! I told ya, I—"

Dorsey raised his hand interrupting him. "A.C., do it for me... our friendship, please."

Adyson sighed and snatched the book.

"Great," Dorsey said. "Peace, bro. With that book you'll make it through the rough times."

"Sure, I will," Adyson said sarcastically, beginning his walk towards freedom.

❧ 4 ❧

HOLIDAY BLUES

Adonyjah Clark lay on the sofa in his contemporary living room. Darkness surrounded him except for the streak of light that escaped through the slats of his vertical blinds. *I'll be glad when tomorrow comes, ending this freakin' holiday season.* "Sorry, Lord," he whispered, feeling guilty about his lack of appreciation for the season.

His thoughts shifted to the sound of keys turning in the front door. *I hope Devon's alone and goes downstairs quietly.* To his dismay, neither came to pass.

"Donnnnay," Devon shouted. Adonyjah lay quietly. "Yo man, I saw your truck outside."

He heard footsteps go downstairs as Devon ascended the stairs to his level, Adonyjah quickly answered, "Wha's up, D?"

"Why you lying in the dark, man?"

Adonyjah ignored his question. "Wha's up?"

"Why you lying in the dark? You okay?" He flipped the light switch. "What's goin' on, Adonyjah?"

Adonyjah sat up, agitated. "Dang, Devon, can't a man just lay quietly? Just go downstairs."

"You're ok? I've never known you to—"

"Go downstairs and leave me alone," Adonyjah snapped through gritted teeth.

Devon spun around and stormed down the stairs. "I was just tryna help," he shouted.

Devon Sherman and Adonyjah had been friends since first grade—Sister Francis' class. Their love for playing pranks, and their respect for the code of secrecy, bonded them for life.

Devon was an only child, so his parents enjoyed having Adonyjah at their house as company for him. Adonyjah loved spending time at the Shermans'. they played games, ate dinner together and had story time. It was a peaceful home to Adonyjah; one he would never have known otherwise.

Adonyjah could hear Devon complaining to Trazie, "Screw you." He was annoyed that Devon had come home and within seconds had transformed his already-frustrated state of mind into an agitated one. *Devon never respects the privacy of someone's mental space.*

Adonyjah rubbed his forehead as if to push his worries out of his mind. His brother Adyson coming home had had him concerned for three months. With tomorrow being his release, it preoccupied his whole existence. *How can I share this with anyone? Who would understand that I love my brother, but I'm afraid of who he is? Is Adyson even capable of change?* In the overexertion of his mind, Adonyjah fell asleep. His mind drifted toward a place in time he avoided when he was awake, a time filled with anguish. He turned on his back, his arm stretched across his forehead.

He was the eldest of Avery and ZaBryna Clark's six children, and the mediator of his family from the time he was old enough to walk. As far back as he could recall, his father, a martial arts instructor, would come home drunk and beat his mother and him when he jumped in to protect her. ZaBryna would push Adonyjah out of the way, but he would lunge back in front of her, swinging his tiny arms to protect her.

There were times he could remember sitting at the table with his mother and his year-old-twin siblings, Adyson and Adryanah. His father would come home after spending the night out and would berate ZaBryna. He would attempt to pick an argument, hoping she would indulge him, but she would avoid those arguments by remaining quiet, keeping the house clean and the children out of his way, correcting any other flaws he found with how she ran the house.

Adonyjah frowned, shaking his foot nervously. The tension and the chaos were always unbearable in that house. He clearly understood the outcome of the Clark children.

He wouldn't involve himself in serious relationships. In his twenty-eight years of life he had one serious relationship: his high school sweetheart, Gevonda Harizon. They dated for fifteen years and were planning for their wedding when Gevonda was killed in a car accident. Her parents were given custody of their two-year-old daughter, Zabryna Harizon; Adonyjah never saw his child again.

Adonyjah understood Gevonda's parents' assumption that they were protecting their grandchild, based on what they knew about the Clark family, but Zabryna (Queenie) deserved to know her daddy. He loved his little girl, and he was a good father. Adonyjah's tears slid down his face in his sleep as he shook his head to escape the memories of his ultimate losses.

Adyson, the second child was incarcerated for sexually assaulting Sharon Coleman, a student at his father's karate school.

Adyson relentlessly begged her not to press charges, but Sharon and her parents were adamant. He was due to be released from the correctional facility on New Year's Eve; the root cause of Adonyjah's disrupted spirit.

Adryanah, as much as she loved men, would assault any man who she felt threatened by. She was serving her fifth year of a seven-year sentence for stabbing her children's father, Chaise. She thought he was cheating on her with his estranged wife.

His third sibling, Alyxander, was a petty drug dealer. He was released from jail six months ago, after serving time for possession of cocaine. Adonyjah devoted his spare time to keeping him out of trouble. He got Alyx a job at his firm, Hartford Sans Data Systems, Inc., in the mailroom. He bought a condo for him two blocks from his own home, encouraging him to enroll in school. Alyxander loved to tinker with model cars, so they checked out automotive schools and eventually found classes at a local college. A smile slid across his face as he thought about how well his brother was doing. They had even started to pray together; Aryngton, his youngest brother included, and their conversations about God were becoming more consistent. He hoped success was near for Alyxander, and his thirst for money would be satisfied. Alyxander hated being poor and would do anything to avoid the pitfalls of poverty.

In the depths of his sleep, Adonyjah could feel the tension and headache travel from the nape of his neck, straight through to his forehead. He opened his eyes and rubbed his head, wondering if he could be depressed. *Who in the world wonders if they're depressed?*

He sat up and lay his head on the back on the sofa. His thoughts immediately shot to his youngest siblings, Aryngton and Aryn. He chuckled at how different they were for twins. Aryn was daddy's little princess. Anything she wanted, she got, at any cost. She started the trouble and they all got in trouble. She grew into a prima-donna, wouldn't work but wanted an extravagant lifestyle. She was supported by her boyfriend Jarvis Bonding, a known crack dealer. Her five-year-old son, Zayne lived with her parents.

Aryngton, also known as Stud, the nickname Adonyjah chose for him because he was so much bigger than him, had surprisingly turned out fine; however, he carried the burden of the family, with no clue of how to let go or even say no. At twenty-five, he was a Regional Manager for Marinard Meats. He'd moved back home so that he could help his parents with the three grandchildren.

Adonyjah was so preoccupied with his thoughts, he never heard the doorbell. *I've never seen Stud in a relation—*

"What's going—"Adonyjah shot a surprised look to the steps. "Hey Stud, I was just thinking about you. When did you get here?" Adonyjah sat up, rubbing his eyes.

"I was ringing the bell. You okay?"

"Yeah, just a little headache. Guess I'm thinking too much."

"Wha's wrong?" Aryngton asked, sitting across from his brother.

"I was thinking 'bout you, as a matter of fact."

"Thinking about me gave you a headache? What'd I do?"

"No, fool! You know me and the holidays—especially New Year's—don't do well. So, I was thinking about us, the family, being together tomorrow evening. I'd really just like to stay home and come into the New Year without the drama; ya feel me?"

The look on Aryngton's face responded before he could answer. "What da crap you talkin' about, Donny? You know Adyson's being released from prison tomorrow. As a matter of fact, I came by to ask you to go with me to pick him up."

Forgetting his headache, Adonyjah leaped off the couch, "Oh

no, Stud! I'm sorry bro, I...uh...uh... I can't! C'mon man, that's too much—"

"Adonyjah," Aryngton interrupted, "we're the only two that's got it together. We've got to pull this family together. There's a new generation coming up in the same crap we grew up in. Please go with me; he's our brother." He sighed, bringing his voice to a whisper, "D-man, he needs us."

Adonyjah leaned his head back on the couch, covered his face and rubbed it. He hoped he could wake from this nightmare. Aryngton moved to the couch, sitting quietly next to him. His shoulders slumped, he stared at the floor. "Adonyjah," Aryngton spoke slowly, "you do know we've got to help him, right? He's our brother. Look at Alyxander. Do you think he'd be doing so well today if we hadn't stepped in to direct him when he got out?"

Adonyjah sat up. "Stud, I know you're right; I even feel that as the eldest I need to step up my game as leader, since your father never will." Aryngton ignored the 'your father' comment to avoid Adonyjah steering them away from the subject.

Adonyjah paused for a moment to give his brother time to challenge the comment; when he realized he hadn't trapped him, he continued. "He sexually assaulted someone's daughter, Stud; I've got a baby girl." The tears rolled down his face as he leaned back on the sofa, covering his face.

Aryngton's stomach clenched when Adonyjah mentioned his niece; Zabryna's name was never mentioned. It was like she didn't exist, and that helped all of them to deal with her absence.

He focused back on what Adonyjah was saying, "We all have our issues, but Adyson and Adryanah not only have issues, they're crazy. I'd love to know what craziness went on with those two in ZaBryna's womb. They're like satanic twins."

"Donny," Aryngton interrupted his attempt to stray again,

"pleaaase help me save our brother. Maybe we should go to counseling as a family, so we can try to overcome our past together."

Adonyjah faced his brother and for a moment their eyes locked. Adonyjah stretched his hand and affectionately placed it on the back of his brother's head, popping him.

"Are you crazy? Aw, no, Stud. You think I'm going to sit in a room with some shrink and dem crazy fools you call family, and *pay* for it? Uh-uhn, I'll go with you to get Adyson tomorrow, though," Adonyjah said, getting up to go to the bathroom.

Aryngton rested his head on the back of the sofa, and widened the grin plastered on his face. "Well Lord, thank you; we're going to get Adyson. That's a start!"

5

SOMETHING'S GOT TO CHANGE

ZaBryna had flipped the last pancake when she heard Avery. "Oh please, not now. Please let that man sleep." She scooped the pancakes off the griddle, placed them on a plate and covered it. Hearing a crash from the back room, she rushed down the hall. She burst through the door to an ashtray flying towards her head.

"Where were you?" Avery demanded.

"Avery, what is it?" she asked calmly.

"Where were you, and what took you so long to come when I called you?" he growled.

"I... uhm, was preparing the meals for the day. You know Adyson's gonna be released today and all the children will be over for dinner." She spoke softly so as not to provoke him. "Avery, what do you need?"

"I need to get out this freakin' bed; I need to have my butt bathed and dressed. I neeeeed to eat. Are you stupid? What do you think I need?"

"Avery," ZaBryna's voice was gentle, "it's four in the morning; it's too early for you to get up. I'm sorry I woke you."

"Well then, bring your tail back to bed, since it's not time to get up."

"Please Avery, I have too much to do and need to get things started before you and the kids get up. If you want coffee, I can bring you some."

"Did I ask for coffee?" Avery snapped.

She looked around the room to see what damage he had done, and then snatched up the books, water pitcher and cup he had thrown. Ignoring his last comment, she started towards the door mumbling, "I'm going to get some paper towels to get up that mess you made."

Her abrupt departure startled Avery. *Did she have an attitude?* "Witch, I'll deal with you later!"

ZaBryna threw the cup in the sink, rinsed out the pitcher, and filled it with cold water from the fridge, then reaching for a clean glass, she stumbled and dropped the pitcher.

"Crap," she shouted, "I hate my life!" Avery's stroke had taken its toll on her. She wished she could blame it on his health, but she couldn't. Her husband was just evil.

They had been married thirty-one years; twenty-nine years too many. Far removed from the present, the water on the bedroom carpet, the broken glass on the kitchen floor, and Avery screaming his lungs out all faded away, as she unconsciously pulled out the chair wondering, *How did I get here?*

ZaBryna had met Avery during her freshman year in high school. He followed her home every day trying to get her to go to the ice cream shop with him. Every day she turned him down, telling him he wasn't her type.

After three years of pursuit, she fell prey to his coercion, and went with him to his uncle's party. She wasn't interested in Avery as a boyfriend, but she liked him as a friend. The two enjoyed each other's company and shared common interests. He was a brown belt at his uncle's karate school, and she was a green belt at Mid-Brook Karate School.

ZaBryna's thoughts were interrupted by the footsteps coming near her. She spun around to find Aryngton standing behind her. "Oh, Stud, you scared me."

"Hey Breena, sorry I scared you." Aryngton could see the stress etched across his mother's face; her eyes looked weary. She was aging, her beauty challenged by the circumstances of her life. "What's wrong?"

"Nothin' baby, I just have so much to do, and Avery's giving me a rough time."

"What's he doin' up so early?" Aryngton asked.

"He insisted last night that I sleep in the room with him; I must've woke him when I got up. Let me get this stuff to him and clean up that mess he made. Hopefully, he's gone back to sleep." ZaBryna snatched the roll of paper towels off the counter, placed it under her arm, picked up the new pitcher, and the clean cup. When she turned, Aryngton pulled her into his arms and held her.

He took the pitcher, cup and paper towels from her, and started walking back to his father's room. "Breena, take care of the food; let me deal with Avery today." Before she could challenge him, he was gone.

Aryngton opened the door slowly and tiptoed to his father's nightstand, placing the pitcher and cup down. He was looking for the wet spot, when he was interrupted by his father's growl. "Where were you?"

"Hey Pops, it's me, Stud," Aryngton said, sounding jovial.

"Where's your mother, and don't call me Pops," Avery retorted.

"Breena's in the kitchen cooking. You know today's New Year's Eve, right? Adyson's coming home. Adonyjah and I are going to pick him up this afternoon. Would you like to go?"

"I know it's New Year's Eve. I'm paralyzed, not stupid, boy," Avery snarled.

Aryngton never responded to Avery's meanness. "Pops, ZaBryna needs cooperation today. She has a lot of things to do to make sure you and the kids' needs are met. So, this morning I'll assist you with anything you need. If you want to go, we can get some lunch, and then enjoy the day out—all the men. We've never done that before."

"First of all, you need to stop calling me Pops; my name's Avery. Second, it was your mother's decision to take in them stupid kids. If she hadn't, she'd only have me to care for and the house would stay clean. Third, I'm not going anywhere with you and Adonyjah. It's New Year's Eve, as you pointed out; I should be home with my wife. And last, I don't want Adyson here; he's a disgrace. Now go and get my wife!" Avery demanded.

Aryngton started to walk to the door, then stopped. "Avery, do you need to use the bathroom?"

"My wife can do that, along with getting me bathed and dressed," Avery retorted.

Aryngton walked towards the trashcan in the kitchen with his usual calm demeanor.

"Was he angry?" ZaBryna inquired.

"No, he's asleep. I'll check on him in thirty minutes," Aryngton lied. "What else do you need me to do?" he asked.

Before ZaBryna could answer, he started filling the kitchen

sink with hot water. "I'll make the sweet potatoes when I finish these dishes."

"Aryngton Clark, what have I done to deserve your assistance this morning?" ZaBryna smiled proudly at him.

"Hey, stop being so suspicious," Aryngton teased. "Can't a son just help his mother?"

"Baby, you know I think it's wonderful. I appreciate it, but don't you have better things to do, than be in the kitchen with me?"

"It's five-thirty in the morning. What else would I be doing?"

"Uh, let's see... sleeping?" ZaBryna playfully responded.

"Breen, it's gonna to be a long day, and I wanna help."

"Well, I do appreciate it. The kids will probably wake up in another two hours; so, your assistance will help me tremendously."

"Good morning, am I late?" Adonyjah greeted, taking off his coat, and walking over to kiss his mother. Startled, ZaBryna grabbed her chest with one hand, and wrapped the other one around Adonyjah's waist. "What are you doing here so early?" She tried to hide her concern while the smile stayed plastered across her face.

"Can't a man hang out with his mother and brother?" He reached over to shake Aryngton's hand. "I was in the neighbor-hood"—Adonyjah paused, throwing his coat out the doorway —"and thought I'd stop by."

ZaBryna gave a hearty laugh. "Boy, go hang your coat up."

"Don't you go worrying about my coat, just give your eldest child some love," he said, hugging her and spinning her around, so that her back was to the door. Aryngton could hardly compose himself with the excitement of his brother's and his surprise.

Adonyjah was dancing with his mother to the music in his head, and Aryngton was apparently listening.

When he spun ZaBryna around, Alyxander was dancing behind her. ZaBryna squealed, and cheerfully hit him in his chest.

"Wait, wait." She pushed Adonyjah off her. "What's going on? Why are you all here?" Confusion immediately replaced her smile; her eyes filled with tears.

"Breena," Adonyjah interrupted, "everything's fine."

"Why are you here?" ZaBryna asked slowly.

Adonyjah sat her down on the chair. "Breena, nothing's wrong, we just want to help you. Aryngton's going to take the kids to the movies around noon. We hired someone to come and stay with Avery this morning, then you, Stud, Devon, Zavian and me are going to pick up Adyson later this afternoon. Maybe Avery can go. Aryn will be here later to do the girly things with you."

"Aryn?" ZaBryna questioned.

"Yep, she will be here in a few hours to take you out."

"Oh my God, that's wonderful... but your father isn't going to allow me to go out, or someone to come and care for him."

"Allow? Avery's in no position to allow or not allow anything. This isn't even about him; this is about you, Bre." Alyxander scowled.

"Now you all know how your father is—" Aryngton raised his hands and cut his mother off. "Ma," he asserted, "like Alyx said, this isn't about Avery."

"Since his stroke we've allowed him to continue dictating what will and won't take place, so it has been all about him. We're welcoming in a new year and it's time to get this house and this family in order. It's time for you to catch a break," Alyxander said.

ZaBryna looked at the clock on the microwave. "Wow, I gotta check on Avery."

Adonyjah stopped her. "I'll go and check on him. Is it time for him to get bathed and dressed?"

"If he's up I can do it now and get it over with," ZaBryna replied.

"No, Alyx and I'll take care of Avery. You and Stud have the kitchen."

"Adonyjah, Avery isn't going to let you bathe him. He's going to get upset," ZaBryna challenged.

"He'll get over it," Alyxander said.

ZaBryna was still sitting when they walked away. "Stud, what's going on? I don't want any problems; I've gotta live with this man." ZaBryna said, looking at her son through concerned eyes. She was petrified.

Aryngton sat at the table next to his mother, grasping her hands. "Breena, nothing's going on. It's been three years since Avery's stroke. You have cared for him every day without a break; you have taken care of your three grandchildren since each of them came home from the hospital and you have never had a moment's rest. No vacation, no pampering and no time for yourself since we were born. Adonyjah, Alyxander, Aryn, Devon, Zavian and I are concerned about you and so we've decided that there need to be some changes."

The tears began to stream down ZaBryna's face. Aryngton grabbed a paper towel and gently wiped his mother's face. "Breena, you can't keep living with all this stress; you need help. Who'll take care of you if you get sick? You're our mother. Let us help you. This time we're not taking no for an answer."

"You all know I appreciate what you're doing, but Avery's a difficult man and I don't want him to feel he's being stripped from being head of this household. I know it seems like he's hateful and

39

domineering. I just don't see—" Aryngton put his finger over her lips, stopping her.

"Breena, Avery has ruled this house for as long as I can remember. He's a mean arrogant man who doesn't care about anyone but himself. Look Breena," he said compassionately, "Aryn will be here in three hours to pick you up and later this morning to talk to Avery before everyone gets here. She's the only one he listens to and fears." They both laughed. "It's gonna be okay; trust me. Okay?"

Breena wiped her eyes and stood up, hoping to grasp the confidence her children possessed. She knew they weren't afraid of Avery, and together maybe they could make changes. "I do trust you all. I know none of you would put me in harm's way. I just don't want this house to turn into a war zone, okay?" she finalized, still sniffling.

"Good morning, Avery!" Adonyjah and Alyxander sang in harmony.

"What are you two doing here so early?"

"We came to help you get ready for the day," Adonyjah said, grinning. He knew his father would be difficult, which was why he and Alyxander were assigned the task.

"I don't know what kinda crap y'all got going on, but I want my wife in here *now*," Avery demanded.

"Breena's cooking, so you're stuck with me and Donny. Hey, do you want to go with us to get Adyson this afternoon?" Alyxander asked.

"Aryngton already asked me that; I said no. I don't want him living here either. Now go and get my wife," Avery snarled.

Adonyjah went into the master bathroom to set up for Avery's bath. He returned to the bedroom and took out Avery's clothes, placing them neatly on the bed. He could feel the pounding in his head building. He already knew Avery wasn't going to allow them to bathe and dress him. He also knew when Alyxander swiftly took over the conversation, Avery wouldn't have a choice.

Alyxander had confided in Adonyjah, Aryngton and Aryn that his mother's freedom was set for the first day of 2010. He'd complained for the last two years about Breena's life, the guilt he felt for doing nothing to help her and it was time to change all of that.

Alyxander gathered the pillows on the bed, propping Avery into a partial-sitting position. He pulled the chair stationed by the door up to Avery's bed and sat down. Adonyjah stood in the doorway with his arms crossed, allowing Alyxander to lead.

His palms were sweaty as he watched his younger brother sit quietly, staring at their father. When Alyxander spoke, his voice was steady and a pitch above a whisper. "Avery, when you finish screaming, I'll talk, but I won't get ZaBryna until you've heard me out."

ADONYJAH LOOKED AT HIS FATHER'S FACE, DISFIGURED FROM the hate that had consumed him for years; the veins in his temples were pulsating and his eyes were bulging. He was a frightening sight. *Will this give him another stroke?*

"Hey Alyx, let me holla at you a minute."

Alyxander briefly shifted his attention to Adonyjah. "No," he said, and he turned back to look at his father.

"Avery, Aryn's on her way to pick up my mother. She's taking her out for some personal business."

"What personal business?" Avery snapped.

Alyxander ignored his question and continued, "Donny and I are going to bathe, dress and feed you this morning. We've hired a nurse who'll begin working with you today, assisting you with all your needs."

"Whhhat?" Avery interrupted again. "Wait a freakin' minute!"

Alyxander continued talking as if Avery hadn't said a word. "We have an hour-and-a-half to get you presentable and fed. Stud'll take the kids to the park this morning while Donny and I finish setting up for tonight's dinner. Breena's going with us later, to pick up Ady—"

"ZaBryna isn't going anywhere. Do you hear me? Now get my wife in here," Avery snarled.

Alyxander ignored Avery again and continued, "Breena's going with us to pick up Adyson; you're welcome to come. We'll leave around three; so, think about it and let us know." Alyxander got up, put the chair back by the door and opened Avery's wheelchair.

Alyxander's actions were swift, confident and frightening, forcing Avery to resign from fighting. For the first time in his life, he experienced fear of the loss of power. Alyxander pushed his arms under Avery's armpits, scooting him to the edge of the bed and sliding him into the wheelchair. Adonyjah stood in disbelief at his father's resignation.

Avery realized he wasn't going to see his wife until he cooperated, so he surrendered himself to their agenda. His mind was racing as he felt Adonyjah lift him onto his shower chair. He submitted to the warm water running over him while Adonyjah washed him. His mind reeled with the possibilities of what could be going on with ZaBryna. *Were his children holding her against her will, or was she going along with their plan to overthrow him?*

She never brought my coffee. She said she'd be right back; but instead,

Aryngton came. Where does he fit into this picture? He's the weakest one. Where is he now? Adonyjah dried him off, and began lotioning him.

"Can Aryngton dress me?" Avery forced himself to sound polite.

Adonyjah gave Alyxander an inquiring look, but before he could answer, Alyxander responded, "Stud's cooking, but you'll see him when you go down for breakfast."

"That's okay, I'll eat in my room," Avery snapped.

"Your room needs to be cleaned, so you'll eat with us," Alyxander retorted. Adonyjah finished tying Avery's shoes, and Alyxander moved him to the wheelchair, taking him to the kitchen.

❦ 6 ❦

DETHRONED

"Trazie, it's almost seven-thirty, we're going to be late. Get up," Devon demanded. "Why do we always have to be late?"

"The question is, why are we goin' to this crap?" Trazie responded, raising himself up on his elbow. "Devon, I can't stand Avery Clark; you know this. He looks down on our lifestyle; he hates his wife, children, grandchildren, life; shall I go on? He was this way before the stroke. Plus, you're supposed to be angry with Adonyjah, or did you forget that?"

Devon took a deep breath after pulling his striped Polo shirt over his head; he stopped to stare at Trazie. "Tre, going today isn't about Avery, it's for Breena. All the kids are pulling together to help her today. I was upset with Donny yesterday; I don't have time to hold grudges."

"Hmmm, so then I guess the question is, did *Donny* get over it? I think he's jealous of our relationship."

"Tre, I'm not trying to argue with you this morning. If you don't want to go, just say so; stop trying to ruin the day."

"That's it? That's all I've gotta do? Shoot, you should've said that when you woke me. I'm not going." Devon took his watch off the dresser, put it on his wrist and left the room.

⌘

"LORD, PLEASE LET THERE BE PEACE THIS MORNING," DEVON quickly prayed, ringing the doorbell.

"Hey Uncle D," greeted an enthusiastic Zayne, who was always jovial, no matter what was going on in his young life.

"Hey, Uncle Zayne," Devon chimed, picking up Zayne, pretending he was an airplane. "Where's ever'body?"

"How come you call me Uncle Zayne? I'm too little to be your uncle."

"You are? I thought you were twenty-five."

"I'm not twenty-five, I'm five." Zayne giggled as Devon carried him to the kitchen where the family was.

"Fam, what's up?"

"Hey, Devon." Adonyjah reached over Aryn to grab his hand, and hug him.

"Dang, Donny, you can't see me here?" Aryn yelled.

"Gurl, please, I didn't touch you. Dev, about yesterday; I... uh, I—"

"Don't sweat it, man," Devon interrupted. "You straight?"

"Yeah, but I was out of line; I'm sorry. You know I just don't do well with these holidays."

Devon walked around the table, and hugged everyone. "Where's Avery? He feelin' okay?"

"He's fine," ZaBryna responded.

"Alyxander's back there schooling his dumb behind," Aryn replied, snidely.

"Uncle Stud, aren't we going to see that *Princess* movie, today?"

"No one wants to see that stupid girly movie, Sami," Zayne interrupted.

"Yeah," added Savyion, "we gonna see Alvin and his brothers, right?" Both boys pleaded.

"Uncue, you said you gonna take me to see the Princess," Symaya whined.

"Girl, you're outnumbered by the boys, so you gonna have to wait till it comes to DVD," Aryn interjected. Symaya dropped her head and cried.

"And don't start cryin' either," threatened Aryn, "you c—

"Leave her alone, Aryn," Adonyjah interrupted. "She has a right to be upset if she was promised something, and now isn't getting it."

"Samy, Uncle Donny will take you tomorrow to see the Princess if you go with the boys today, to see Alvin."

"Why do the boys get to go first to see dere movie?" she cried.

Adonyjah picked her up from the table and hugged her. "How many pancakes do you want?"

"Two." she exclaimed, showing him her two fingers.

"How many bacons?"

"Four."

"I want four bacons too," Sayvion chimed.

"I want six bacons," Zayne yelled.

"Oh no," Adonyjah said. "You're going to see the movie you want to see today. Princess Samy can't see her movie, so this is your way of thanking her."

Zayne thought for a minute and asked," So if we go see her movie today, we can get a lot of bacons?"

"Where's this going, Mr. Psychologist?" Devon teased.

"That's what I wanna know," Aryngton said, scooting himself up on the counter.

Adonyjah was thinking of an answer. "Huh, Uncle Donny?" Zayne inquired.

"Yep, you sure do. You can have four bacons and two pancakes if you go see the Princess movie first."

Zayne and Sayvion could hardly stay in their seats. "We'll go see the Princess today, Uncle Donny."

WHEN SYMAYA THOUGHT THEY WOULD WIN, SHE WRAPPED HER arms around her uncle's neck and whispered, "I'll go see Alvin and his brodders."

"We have a winner," shouted Adonyjah, "Symaya will escort Uncle Aryngton, Zayne and Sayvion to see Alvin. It's settled." He took a bow.

"Aw, man," shouted Zayne and Sayvian.

Aryngton, Devon, ZaBryna, and Adonyjah gave her a round of applause, and then he placed the excited Symaya back in her seat.

Zayne and Sayvion shouted, "That's not fair, we want more bacon."

"Now how's that fair to these boys that she gets four pieces of bacon, and they only get two?" Aryn asked, annoyed.

"When they finish what's on their plates they can have more," Adonyjah snarled.

"BOYS, EAT WHAT'S ON YOUR PLATE, AND THEN YOU CAN HAVE more." ZaBryna instructed them.

"GOOD MORNING, FAMILY," ALYXANDER SAID AS HE WALKED IN the kitchen. "Avery wants to join us for breakfast."

Symaya and Sayvion jumped out of their chairs, running to greet their grandfather, but before they could get close, Avery raised his hands, stopping them. Alyxander leaned over and whispered in his ear, causing Avery's face to cringe. He reached out his hand to them and allowed them to come to the side of his wheelchair and hug him.

"Why don't we eat in the dining room," ZaBryna suggested, removing two chairs from the dining room table, making room for Avery's wheelchair.

"Yeah," agreed Zayne, "we never get to play in there. I'm sitting next to Breena."

"No, *I'm* sitting next to Breena," Symaya whined.

"I said it first," argued Zayne.

"Zayne, let her sit next to Breena; she's younger," Adonyjah said.

"What? Symaya wasn't even thinking about sitting next to Breena, until Zayne said he wanted to," Alyxander interjected. "Zayne sit next to your grandmother. Samy you can sit next to your auntie." His voice was gentle, but firm.

"No, I wanna sit next to Breena," Symaya cried, stomping her feet and folding her arms in protest. Alyxander stooped down to her level, just as Adonyjah was going to pick her up. "Samy, you can sit next to Aryn or Donny; see, he's right here to pick you up." Alyx looked up at Adonyjah. "If you don't want to do that you can sit anyplace you want. Avery and Zayne are sitting next to Breena."

"I wanna sit next to Breena," she yelled.

"Zayne, get up and let your cousin sit next to her grandmother, so she can shut up," Avery scolded.

"No. Bless the food; Symaya and I need to talk." Alyxander scooped her up and went to her room. Adonyjah could barely hide his annoyance with Alyxander. *It's not a big deal, all Zayne had to do was move and let the baby sit next to her grandmother.*

"You know he's right; Samy's getting out of hand. She's starting to become like you-know-who." Devon interrupted his thoughts.

"She's a baby, Devon; she doesn't know what she's doing."

"Donny, you're the one that doesn't know what she's doing because your blind love for Queenie causes you to compensate for Symaya's negative behavior. That's not helping her. Losing both her parents and living in this house are strikes against her; so, allowing her to manipulate us won't help her either. You wouldn't have let Queenie get away with it."

"I don't wanna talk about this anymore," Adonyjah said, feeling his anger turning on Devon. He knew Devon was right and he couldn't stand too much conversation involving his daughter. Adonyjah knew he was Symaya's puppet, especially now that his daughter was gone.

"Samy, you can sit by Uncle Donny; *orrrrrrr*, you can sit in your room until you stop crying. Now you tell Uncle Alyx what you want to do?"

Samy stood with her mouth poked out, tears rolling down her face, leaning against the wall. "I wanna sit next to Breena," she whimpered.

"That's not the question; Zayne and Avery are sitting next to her. Next time we eat in the dining room, you can sit next to Breena. But today you're going to sit next to someone else, or sit in your room. Now I'm hungry and my food's getting cold; so, when I count to three, you have to tell me what you're going to do, okay?"

"Onne, tttttttwwoo, ttttttthrrrrrreeeee," he sang. "Do you wanna sit in your room?" Symaya shook her head, no.

"Do you wanna sit next to Auntie Aryn?" she shook her head no, again.

"Do you wanna sit next to me?" she smiled hesitantly, shaking her head from side-to-side.

"You don't wanna sit next to me, your handsome, wonderful, Uncle-Alyx?" She apprehensively shook her head, no. Alyx knew she was going to pick Donny, so he did a drum roll with his mouth, and excitedly asked, "Do ya wanna sit next to Uncle Donny?"

She nodded her head up and down with the same excitement he asked the question. Then he whispered, pretending that someone was trying to steal their secret. "Go to Uncle Donny, and say, 'I got you, babe'!"

She ran into the dining room, jumped on Adonyjah, giggled her version of *I got you babe,* climbed in his lap, reached in his plate and grabbed his bacon.

"Hey." He joined in her little joke and hugged her. Everyone shifted their seat to include her and Alyxander. Donny shot Alyx a look of embarrassment; Alyxander gave him a thumbs up. He knew his brother was pissed with him, but he also knew he'd do everything he could to make sure his niece didn't turn out like his sisters.

⬥

ZaBryna reached her hand across the table to stop Paul when he began clearing the table. "I'll do that; relax."

"Breena, Paul's fine; *you* relax," Aryngton said, looking at his watch to make sure their meeting began on time.

"Hey family," greeted Zavion Bennings, walking into the dining room. "What's up?"

"Hey, Zav," everyone greeted.

"C'mon kids." The boys jumped out of their seats to join Zavion, but Samy held on to Adonyjah. Zavion pretended he had something in his pocket to show them, and Symaya leaped into his arms to see it first. "It always works." He laughed.

Paul cleared the table completely and returned to the kitchen.

"Well, I'll see you all later," Devon said, standing up."

"Where you going?" Alyxander asked.

"Home."

"Man, sit down; you know we've got a meeting this morning," Adonyjah interjected.

"I thought it was just you guys," Devon whispered, shooting a suspicious eye at Avery.

"He's not family," Avery snapped, "so, he can get out!"

"We need everyone here," Adonyjah argued. "When one of us isn't available, Devon's always stepped in; he's family."

"Not to me; he's a queer," Avery snarled.

"Avery," ZaBryna scolded, "this child has been one of ours since the children were little."

"No one's talkin' to you. I didn't need another child; I had enough of these fools to feed—"

"Hold it." Alyxander stood up. "We've got one hour for this meeting; it won't be wasted arguing. Adonyjah, Aryngton and I asked Devon to be here. He's visited Adyson and Adryanah since they've been incarcerated, and he takes the kids out to help ZaBryna; so, he's got every right to be here."

"ZaBryna don't need no help," Avery argued.

Aryngton began fidgeting; he could feel the stress beginning to embrace his shoulders and chest. *Why in the world did they want this meeting with Avery? Now what are we gonna do?*

"Avery, you can either cooperate, or be removed from this meeting. Devon stays." Alyxander said firmly.

"Who you talking to, Alyxander?" Avery shouted. "Dis *my* house."

"Alyxander, baby," ZaBryna intervened, to calm things down.

"No, Breena!" Alyxander interrupted.

"Excuse me," Paul interjected, "I don't mean to interfere but maybe you might wanna pray—"

"Pray! Ain't gonna be no prayin' up in here, so go wash the dishes and stay out of our business; you're the help!" Avery shouted.

"This is why I said this wasn't a good idea." Adonyjah directed his comment to Alyxander.

"Alyx, I ain't got time for this," Aryn interjected. "You ready to go, Breena?"

"ZaBryna, ain't goin' nowhere," Avery yelled.

"Who you yellin' at, ole man?" Aryn shouted, standing up to confront her father.

"Wait a doggone minute; everybody shut up," Alyxander shouted jumping to his feet. "Shut up, *now*."

"Alyx, you done lost your mind, telling me to shut up." Aryn scowled.

"Aryn," Alexander whispered, snapping his head in her direction; his teeth clenched, his eyes piercing through her, "please sit down and be quiet."

All eyes focused solely on Alyxander. Devon bowed his head, closed his eyes, and prayed for order. Adonyjah shook his head in defeat; he knew it was an impossible task to get his family on the same page.

Devon stood up. *Someone must support Alyx,* he thought. "Look, the purpose of today's meeting is for us to become a better support system to each other. I know I'm not your biological child, Avery; but," Devon sighed, "you're the only family I have with my mom and dad having passed." He stopped for a few seconds to acknowledge them. Almost immediately the tension dissolved among the siblings.

"Now," Devon spoke slowly, not knowing when Avery would attack again, "Adyson's coming home today, and there are concerns about his release. Our goals should be to help him transition into society; set him up with a place to live, get him employed, and in an educational program. Devon looked down at the table to see if he had left an imprint. He took what seemed to be his first breath since he began talking. *How did I become the speaker? What happened to Alyxander, the leader of this whole campaign?*

He looked around and saw everyone staring at him in disbelief. Alyxander reached over, stood up, grabbed his hand, and hugged him. "Well done, brothah, I don't know who jumped in you but you ain't *never* been this bold. Devon's right, we need a change, and it starts today to end the years of the chaos this family has endured," Alyxander concluded.

Devon raised his hand to interject. "I was thinking it would be nice if all of us went to pick up Adyson. You know, do something he wouldn't expect."

"No!" Aryn shouted. "You all act like Adyson did nothing wrong. I despise the fact that he's even getting out. I won't go, and neither will my son."

"I stand with my daughter," Avery chimed in.

"It was just a suggestion. none of us are proud of what Adyson did; helping him adjust doesn't mean we condone his actions. If he's going to stay out of trouble and turn his life around, he's going to need help."

"Yeah, well I'm still pissed too, but no matter how long I stay angry, he's still my brother, and I hope if I'd fall, my family would help me get back on my feet," Aryngton said.

"I was upset with Alyx the other day because he sent Aryngton to ask me to go with him, but then he reminded me of where Alyx was. He could've easily been back in jail, had it not been for us stepping in to help him," Adonyjah said.

Alyxander continued, "Aryn, this family has been messed up all our lives and only we can change it. If Adyson comes out acting the fool, the consequences will be on him. Your choices in life may not have caused as much pain to others as Adyson's, but your actions did cause pain and still do. Everyone has stepped up to help raise Zayne, because we love you; we're family."

"Where would any of those kids be if ZaBryna and Aryngton hadn't stepped up to care for them? Shoot, where would you be every time you and that idiot, Jarvis go through your adolescent phases?" Adonyjah continued.

"We have two siblings incarcerated; none of us should be content with that," Alyxander said.

The tears rolled down Alyxander's face; he took a deep breath, trying to control himself. "Look, I was in prison for three months before Adonyjah answered any of my letters. The only one who wrote me, prior to him, was Devon. Every night, I would read those letters; they gave me strength to do the next day."

"The last two months I served I started seeing hope for when I got out of there. Adonyjah, Devon, Zavian and Aryngton told me they'd help me get on my feet, but I had to promise to stay away from selling drugs. Adonyjah got me the job, and went with me to enroll in school. They bought the condo, my clothes, and my computer. How could I break my promise when they took a chance on me, even when I didn't want to take a chance on myself? For the first time in my life, I felt secure. That is why I feel we should extend ourselves to our siblings. We could start with Adyson since he's being released and then start communication with Adryanah; maybe we could take turns visiting her."

Aryn was still shaking her head no. "I can't, both Adyson and Adryanah are crazy, you know that. Adryanah's a raggedy witch! They're both too hardheaded. And where's Adyson gonna live? Who will hire a sexual—"

"Aryn," Alyxander interrupted, "he's our brother. Jarvis has screwed you over repeatedly, yet you can always run your simple butt around to help him and the rest of his cruddy family."

"Jarvis didn't sexually assault anyone, Alyx," Aryn defended.

"No, he didn't," Adonyjah interjected. "He just kills young women, men, children, and unborn babies, with that crack he sells."

Aryn jumped out of her seat and charged at Adonyjah, "What did you say about my man?" she snarled.

"I said he kills people, which makes him, no betta than Adyson. Shoot, you're just as guilty as Jarvis, since you condone his lifestyle." Adonyjah repeated himself; catching Aryn's hand, before she made contact with his face. "What's the matter, Aryn, the truth too much for you?"

"Let her go, Adonyjah," Avery snarled. "Long as you live don't you ever put your hand on my daughter; you hear me?"

"You've been beating my mother for as long as I can remember; you got the nerve to reprimand me for protecting myself from my own sister?" Adonyjah scowled.

"Stop. *Stop it*," Alyxander yelled. "Look, it's getting late and we've accomplished nothing in the last forty-five minutes. Aryn, if you don't wanna go, we can't force you."

"I'M GONNA TAKE THE KIDS TO THE PARK BEFORE WE GO TO THE movies. I'll take them to an early show and then get them some lunch," Aryngton said, hoping Zavian and the kids would return soon from their walk. "We'll meet back here at about three."

"My son's not going." Aryn said, firmly.

"That's fine; you just need to make yourself available to care for him, 'cause Breena's going," Alyxander replied.

"ZaBryna," Avery shouted, "you won't be going anywhere this afternoon. Do you hear me?"

"Avery, if you can stop her from going, then she won't be going; other than that, plan your afternoon to be in the company of Paul."

7

A NEW BEGINNING

This should be the happiest day of my life, but I can't even enjoy it 'cause I'm alone, Adyson thought, walking towards the transportation depot. He had a few bucks in his pocket and needed to find a shelter; his heart was also tormented by the holiday. He had no intention of seeing or calling anyone; they couldn't care less about him, anyway.

His stride grew as his anger increased inside him. They all think they're perfect; they act like I'm not their blood. I know that's why they didn't communicate with or visit me. I wish Dev didn't live with Adonyjah; I'd probably have a place to stay. Devon wasn't even blood; yet, he was more brother than any one of them fools. I know he'd let me stay with him, if he could.

The metal gates slid open; Adyson stepped out into a new life. This is my time to start over; his eyes became misty. Man up, fool; you're out and there's no time for bathing in all this negativity and sorrow, he scolded himself. I've gotta git it together. My first and most impor-

tant goal will be to stay outta prison; yeah, that's my plan. Shoot, I ain't gonna date, I ain't even gonna look at a woman.

Five feet from the transportation stand, he saw a black Escalade and silver Pathfinder coming towards him. The black truck pulled up right in front of him. He frowned. *This fool's going to sit in front of me, and the other idiot followed behind him. Now, if the freakin bus comes, I gotta walk past both these fools. This is how people end up in jail; always some fool pissing you off.*

Adyson stepped back to the seating area, the frown still plastered on his face. *I've gotta be positive and not let crap piss me off so easily.* Preoccupied with his bungled thoughts, he never noticed the front passenger side window was down; he sat staring right through it.

"HELLO, SON," ZABRYNA SAID, GETTING OUT OF THE TRUCK. "Come, give your momma a hug, baby."

"Breena," he shouted, tears quickly rolled down his cheeks as he rushed to her, picked her up off the ground, spun her around and then put her back down. "You look beautiful. I can't believe you're here, never would've thought Avery would let you come." He tried to stop his rambling but couldn't; he was enthralled with the presence of his mother.

"Yo man, all you see is Breena?" Adonyjah teased, walking around the front of the truck.

"Donny," Adyson exclaimed.

The back doors swung open and Aryngton stepped out. "Bro, how are you?" he asked, turning to lift Symaya, and Sayvion out. Zayne followed behind, climbing over the back seat and jumping out.

Adyson stepped away from everyone; he could no longer compose himself. "I'm sorry, I uh... uhm just, I jus—"

"Spit it out, dude!" Alyxander demanded, climbing out the Pathfinder parked behind Adonyjah's Escalade. Devon came from the driver's side. Then the back doors of Devon's truck flew open and Zavian and Aryn stepped out.

"Thank you. Thank you. I can't tell you what this means to me. I didn't know where I was gonna go and still don't, but you all being here makes this a whole lot better." He walked over to Aryn and took her hand. "Ryn, I'm so sorry for destroying your friendship with Sharon. Please forgive me." The tears rolled down Aryn's face. She hadn't expected this from Adyson; she only agreed to come because Breena begged her. "We'll talk," was all she could say. She was afraid to trust Adyson, afraid to believe him. *He could just be caught up in his emotions.*

"Bree, I'm sorry for the embarrassment I caused you, all of you." He swung his arms around to include everyone. "I'm thankful you all found it in your hearts to support my release. Man, I never wanna be incarcerated again. I wanna be a betta person. I was walking through the gates cussing everyone out because I felt none of you would give me another chance. I know that sounds punkish, but I keep thinking I might need some help to make it."

"You've got that," Adonyjah, Aryngton, Alyxander, Devon and Zavian assured him.

"It's gonna be alright, baby," ZaBryna assured him.

"Okay folks, I think we need to head home; we got a dinner to devour," Adonyjah instructed. "Haze," Adonyjah used their nickname for Adyson, "there's room in Devon's truck; you can drive wi—"

"No, Haze," Aryngton interrupted, "ride with ZaBryna; me

and the boys can ride with Devon."

"Yes, come ride with me," ZaBryna insisted.

Adyson walked over and extended his hand; when Devon responded, he pulled him into him and hugged him. "Thanks, big brothah; I know this is all your doing." Devon stepped back, shaking his head, "Actually, it's Alyx's and Aryngton's."

◈

ADYSON SAT BEHIND HIS MOTHER, QUIETLY OBSERVING THE scenery. He watched as the leafless trees swooshed by him and almost immediately caught the sun sneaking away from him.

"Sunset, how beautiful," he mumbled, rubbing his hand on his chin. *It's amazing how much I took for granted.* He could hear Adonyjah, and ZaBryna laughing in the background of his thoughts.

When did my family become so close? They all seemed so, hhmm, family, that's the word I'm looking for, he thought it out in his head slowly, *faammmilly. It's not a bad thang; just too late for me. I'm just glad they came to get me; now I just gotta git myself set up at a shelter and figure o—*

"Adyson, you hungry?" ZaBryna asked, interrupting his thoughts.

"Actually, I'm so sick of eating that nasty food, I don't even think about getting hungry anymore."

"Bro, that's sad." Adonyjah laughed.

"Hey Breena, how's Avery doing?"

"He's okay. He stopped therapy a while back; he said it wasn't helping. Don't seem to wanna do much except sit in the house and you know?"

"What? Drive you crazy?" Adyson laughed.

"Baby, I don't mind; I'm the wife. It's my job to take care

of him."

"Breena," Adonyjah interrupted, wanting to change the subject. He hated that his mother's self-esteem was so challenged. "I'm not gonna stay when we get back to the house. I've got some errands to run. You want me to take Symaya with me, so you can finish up with dinner?"

"No, I'll keep the kids; that way they can bathe early; plus, Aryn and Stud will be there. You know, Haze, your brothers hired someone to take care of Avery today. That's how I was able to come."

"Ohhhhhhhhh, y'all got it like that now?" Adyson teased, pushing Adonyjah's arm.

"I even got my hair and nails done, see?" ZaBryna stuck her fingers in his face like a child. "Aryn picked out the color for my nails, and the style for my hair," she said, turning her head from side to side.

"They look beautiful, Breena, you deserve to be pampered. So, what did Avery say about the new, fantabulous you?" Adyson teased, trying to feel comfortable with them.

"He was sleep when I got back, then we left, so he hasn't seen it yet," she replied nervously.

"I'm sure he's gonna love it; you look beautiful," Adonyjah said, patting her hand to calm her.

"Sssssssoooo, how did Avery do with you going out?" Adyson asked.

"Not good, he's very upset," ZaBryna said, rubbing her forehead. She could not hide the concern in her voice. Adonyjah reached over and grabbed his mother's hand again. "It's gonna be okay, Breena. Avery will adjust; you have nothing to be afraid of."

Adyson sat quietly observing his eldest brother's interaction with their mother; he had spent years hating Adonyjah. He always thought he was too sensitive. A punk, with that touchy, feely, huggy-kissy personality; however, as he watched his brother comforting his mother, he felt strange. The desire to reach forward, wrap his arms around her to assure her Adonyjah was right overwhelmed him. He wanted to say, "It's gonna be alright 'cause ya now got me to protect you," but he couldn't because he couldn't even help himself at this point.

Adonyjah, Alyxander, and Aryngton always had an "express yourself" type relationship with ZaBryna. As far back as he could remember, when they were young his brothers would sit at the kitchen table sharing their thoughts with his mother; they valued her. They'd give her updates on whatever was going on in school and were always concerned with how she was doing. They would get pissed when Avery went on one of his tirades, and hit or cursed at her.

He, on the other hand, understood his father; ever since he was a little boy, Avery would take him and Aryn driving after ZaBryna upset him. He could remember his dad crying in the car, saying he wished ZaBryna would cooperate with him. He always felt so bad for him because Avery had had such a rough childhood as an orphan; his parents died when he was in second grade.

When Avery opened the karate school, ZaBryna would always be late bringing them to class, because she wanted them to finish their homework. No matter what Avery wanted to do, ZaBryna would never comply. He'd hated ZaBryna for as long as he could remember because he thought she was stupid for constantly making his father angry.

His brothers and Adryanah would always end up fighting him and Aryn after each of his parents' disagreements. He couldn't understand what his brothers saw in this woman who spent her life breeding kids, was unemployed, and too stupid to make her husband happy. How hard could it have been? He thought about his sisters, Adryanah and Aryn. They were so different from ZaBryna; they'd slit a man's throat for cursing at them, much less putting a hand on them.

Now here he was looking at this same woman he had despised all his life, and he felt sorry for her. Yet he was so excited that she came with everyone to pick him up. He flashed back to her excitement, showing him her nails and twisting her head to show her new hairdo. He tried to remember when he had ever seen her hair professionally done.

He watched and marveled at this woman, his mother; the woman who had allowed her body to be used to give him life and the tears welled up in his eyes. He thought about Dorsey Sparke and could hear him saying, "*All men are created in God's image, Clark, and when God said, 'all men' he was including women.*" He pulled himself forward in his seat, wrapping his arms around ZaBryna and the front passenger seat and kissed his mother.

"Oh, what did I do to deserve that?"

"For loving me despite everything," Adyson forced out, emotionally.

"You okay back there? Ya need air? I'd think you'd be ecstatic, being a free man," Adonyjah teased.

"I am, I am. You know it's just, I don't have a crystal ball to show me my future. There's a lot I gotta do to start over. I'm just trying to figure out some things."

ZaBryna shifted to her side, to look back at her son, the child she could never protect from himself. She reached her hand over, imitating patting him. "It's going to be okay; just enjoy today, for today. Don't think about tomorrow, because you can't do anything right now about tomorrow. Just take one day at a time."

Adyson smiled. Taking her hands in his, he rubbed them. It

was the first time he'd had such a personal encounter with his mother and he cherished it.

◎❧◎

ALYXANDER OPENED THE PASSENGER DOOR, REACHED FOR HIS mother's hand and helped her step out of the truck. "What time's dinner?" he asked, looking at his watch.

"How about seven-thirty? That'll give everyone two-and-a-half hours to relax, change and get back here. Is that okay with you all?" ZaBryna asked.

"That's fine. Alyxander, Devon and I have a run to make with Zavian, then we can come back and help you," Adonyjah said.

"I think we've got it under control here; y'all just handle your business," Aryngton chimed in.

"Uhm, I think I'm going to take a walk around to check out the neighborhood," Adyson said, handing the sleeping Symaya, to Aryngton.

"Where are you going, man?" Devon asked casually.

"Nowhere special, just wanna go for a little stroll," he replied, wanting to get away from everyone.

"You don't wanna go with us?" Adonyjah inquired.

"Donny, it's not like you invited me, man. I—"

"Look man, I didn't include you because I thought you'd probably wanna spend time with your father," Adonyjah yelled. Alyxander elbowed him.

"I don't believe Avery wants to spend time with me," Adyson retorted. *Why does my relationship with these people always gotta be so uncomfortable? I know they hate me, because I was one of Avery's favorites until I went to jail. Avery always told me he didn't care what I did illegally; just don't get caught.*

"Hey Haze, take a ride with us, then you can stay at my house till it's time for dinner," Zavion suggested to relieve the tension.

"C'mon, brothah," Devon said, putting his arms on Adyson's shoulder. You can ride with me."

Adyson followed Devon to his truck and climbed in. He needed to be alone, to think; sure, today was a holiday, but for him it was the first day of his homelessness. He hated that he had to stay in a shelter. He needed clothes, a job, money; every necessity for survival to keep him out of trouble.

Adyson was happy Devon was still standing outside talking; it gave him a little time to be alone with his thoughts. He closed his eyes for what seemed like a second. When he opened them ZaBryna was vigorously waving her hand, smiling and throwing him kisses as she walked towards the door to her building. Adyson smiled and waved back, wondering what would happen to her once she crossed the threshold to Avery's domain.

"Sorry dude, we are seldom all together; you know: Zavian, Donny, Stud, Alyx, Aryn, you and me being together. Only one missing is Adryanah. Even ZaBryna got a chance to escape from her reality. God is great!"

They pulled off, following Zavian to his house. "I swear I don't know why this fool moved all the way to Clinton. That's why we don't visit his butt." Devon laughed.

"You okay?" Devon shot a look towards Adyson. "For a man who just got his freedom, you ain't lookin' too happy."

"Just got a lot on my mind, really, just probably need to be by myself. For you all, this is New Year's Eve; for me, it's my first day of a whole lot of problems with no solutions," Adyson said.

"Haze man, you're free; that's enough to rejoice about. I don't get it; you have your family behind you."

"Do I?" Adyson snapped, "'Cause as I see it, Donny and you all had plans and I wasn't included. It was only when you people thought I was gonna look for prey that Adonyjah decided he wanted me around so I could be watched."

Devon's anger rose immediately. "Good grief, Adyson, when does it stop with you? Everyone has reached out to you because we want to see you make it, and all you can do is criticize and undermine everyone's actions. There's no ulterior motive behind our actions, Adyson; we just wanna see you succeed. We know you're gonna need some help and support."

"No one has ever excluded you; you've always looked down on your brothers and Adryanah because they had issues with Avery. They're reaching out to you, Haze; can't you see that?"

"Donny wrote me one time, *one time,* Devon. You call that reaching out? Aryngton was the only one who visited occasionally. Alyx, this is the first time I've seen him. You were the only one who visited me regularly."

"*Jesus help him,*" Devon shouted, hitting the steering wheel. "Didn't Donny deposit money into your "spending account" every month? One-hundred-and-fifty dollars, am I right, Adyson?"

"Oh, so what... he went bragging to you?"

"No, a few times he had to borrow the money from me because he had a private investigator looking for Lil Zabryna. When his money was tied up in that, then I would purchase the money orders for him. You know Adonyjah don't brag. Alyx, well shoot, he just got out jail six months ago; he can't help anyone until he can stand on his own. And Aryngton did well to visit you once in a blue moon or occasionally, as you call it; he travels with his job and is practically raising Zayne, Sayvion and Symaya, with ZaBryna. He's stepped up to the plate as father, uncle and care-giver since Avery got sick."

Devon tried to compose himself. "Adyson, your brothers are

reaching out to you because they love you, they wanna help you; they feel if everyone pulls together, you'll be fine. Look at Alyx, he's got his own place, working, goin' to school, enhancin' his spirituality and helped make today possible, not just for you but for ZaBryna. Please don't ruin this for yourself and everyone else."

Adyson stared out the window, absorbing all that Devon had said. *In all the years I've known this brothah, I ain't never seen him pissed off.* "I must really sound like an a-hole that you're raising up on me like this. Look man, I had no intentions of dealing with these people when I got out. They are different from me. Riding home with Adonyjah, I watched him and ZaBryna interact with one another. For a few minutes, I flashed back to how my brothers always were pissed with Avery for the way he treated ZaBryna.

"Today for the first time in my life, I got a chance to look at my mother for the person that she is." He became emotional. "I've never given that woman an ounce of respect; I despised her. Yet she risked the wrath of Avery to come pick me up. How brave was that? Why didn't I know Avery was wrong? Why am I the one so screwed up? I've never been in sync with my brothers, you know that. I just don't b—"

"Adyson, Avery spent a lot of time with you; he brainwashed you. But now you have a chance at a new start, for a change. You can either exclude yourself from everyone like you've always done, or you can try something different—embrace your family. It's up to you, you're my brother; I wanna see you do well. Dude, I don't ever want to visit you with glass plates between us again."

"Me neither, man. That was the longest three years of my life. Look D, I really appreciate what you all did today, coming to pick—"

"But...?" Devon interjected.

"I ain't gonna lie, the support blew me away. I was standing at the shuttle stop, battling everyone in my head. Then two idiots driving SUVs pulled up in front of me"—he paused, shaking his head in disbelief—"and...there was ZaBryna's face looking right at me. I looked right past her. I can't even explain; it's a day I'll never forget and I'll always appreci—"

"But?" Devon repeated.

"I ain't never felt love like I did at —"

"And?" Devon asked.

"C'mon, Devon, give me a break. Why you sweatin' me?"

"I'm trying to understand what you're talking about, Adyson. There's a but somewhere; so, I'm waiting for you to be honest."

"Look, I really need to get away from everybody, be by myself. Everyone's got themselves together. Everyone's got rides; Zavian done bought himself a house, everybody's employed. I don't even have nothing decent to put on for tonight's dinner. I ain't tryin' to bust up this New Year's, for y'all. I gotta get a plan; sitting at the house tonight; ain't gonna do me no good. I need to find a shelter, get a newspaper to job search, set an appointment with the Probation Man; you know what I mean?"

"No I don't. It's a holiday, ain't a flippin thang open, so you ain't gonna accomplish none of what you talkin' about till Monday; that three days away," Devon snapped, "We're going to Zavian's for a few, then you can come home with me until it's time to go to Bree's house."

Pulling up in front of Zavian's house, Devon softened his voice and gently shook Adyson's shoulder. "I'm here for you, man; just take one day at a time. For now embrace today, your first day back into society, because this is... a new beginning!"

❧ 8 ❧

TAKE MY HAND

Marian sat on her living room windowsill feeding Jacinta, watching Zavian. "Uhn-uhn-*uhn*. That's one big piece of black beauty. Jazta, I think I see your new da-da. Mama just gotta get him to turn his head away from that dummy Kenya, and on to me."

"Wait a minute, now. I think I see some more mens." She burped the baby, laid her in the bassinet, and turned off the lights. Zavian, Alyxander, and Adonyjah stood outside waiting for Devon to park. Marian looked over all the possibilities that stood in front of Zavian's house. *Them's some fine-looking dudes; dang, about time some brothas came 'round.*

Just as she was about to get up, her eyes gazed upon Adyson walking towards the house. "Hmm-hmm-hmm, now that's beauty!" She opened her top dresser drawer and took out the binoculars she bought to monitor Zavian a year ago. *Yeah, he's fine, about six-two, look at those dreads. Man, if it weren't so late, I could get a good look at his face. Well, looks like I've gotta pay Mr. Zavian a visit.*

She walked to the phone to call Kenya. "Daannng, that ho went to New York with that stuck up ole Tiffani. Kenya's such an idiot, running behind Tiffani and her tired, dumb, pregnant self. *I don't know what Zavian sees in her; she ain't thinking about him. She's so caught up in doin' it for herself, she act like she's too good for a man. Always talking about not fornicating 'cause it's offensive to God. Pleeeeaaaaaaaase! He's the one that gave us these feelings, so He knows we need to get ours.*

"I'll eventually get Zavian," she whispered, shooting her eyes back across the street, "or at least one of them." Feeling frustrated, she walked to her room and lay across her bed, contemplating what she should do. *Is he having a party and didn't invite me?* She strolled back to the living room and peeped out the window; they were gone.

Briskly she walked to her room and opened her closet to see what she should wear. *He ain't havin' no party without me. He probably invited that fool Kenya; she makes me sick. I only tolerate her because she helps me with these kids. Hope she never has kids; her desperate behind can continue to take care of mine.*

Marian leaned into the closet and pulled out her fuchsia-print, low-cut blouse and black capris. She laid them on the bed, then pulled out her four inch heels from under her bed. She sat down next to her clothes and lit a cigarette, considering how she would make her debut without causing a scene with Zavian. *He always actin' like my visits to his house are unwelcome. Ain't like he got a woman; matter-of-fact, I ain't seen him bring one home since I moved here.*

But tonight that wasn't her concern; she was getting her a man tonight. She gave herself one last look over, checked to see if her children were asleep and headed across the street.

"Zave, give us a tour of your mansion," Alyxander teased.

"Follow me." He walked through the foyer to the moderately decorated kitchen, pointing out his favorite amenities. "Beer, anyone?"

"I'll wait till after the tour," Adonyjah replied.

"Over to my left, the dining room's decorated with a card table and chairs for when I entertain the ladies; to my right, is the family room," he said, stepping down into it. "I call it the stu-di-o; Donny and I installed the DVD sound system. We've gotta try it out soo—"

"Fool, you ain't tried that system, yet?" Adonyjah interrupted.

"Ah no, man! I've been busy; you know I just made partner at the firm. By the time I get home, eat, shower and talk to my honeys, I'm beat. It's hard being a lover."

"Psst, ya know, you may need some lessons on being a lover. By the way, how's Kenya?" Devon teased.

"Not feeling me, that's for sure. If she don't git it together, I'm gonna move on. A brothah can't just keep bein' put on the backburner."

"Ya should've moved on a long time ago. It's goin' on two years you been after her," echoed Alyxander. "She must know all you're after is drawers and so she ain't feelin' you."

"Hey. Hey. Where's all this aggression comin' from? Am I sensing haters in the room?" Zavian teased.

"Man, shut up and let's see the rest of the house," Adonyjah said, then laughed.

They walked up the stairs talking and laughing over each other. When they got to the top of the stairs, Zavian directed them to the master bedroom. "This is the King's suite, don't get jeal—"

Laughter traveled throughout the house; Devon, Alyxander, and Adonyjah were hysterical when they walked in. "Your décor is out of this world," Alyxander remarked, "don't you think Adyson?" Adyson laughed but made no comment; after all, who was he to comment when he had nothing but what was on his back.

"I see y'all ain't feelin' my decorative skills; I'll have you know that my bedroom attire is on order."

Adyson watched in amazement at how they teased one another. This was the first time he had hung with his brothers; he wanted to enjoy it, but he still felt awkward.

"Zave, where's your furniture?" Adonyjah inquired.

"THAT'S WHAT I'M GIVING ADYSON."

"Hold up," Adyson demanded. "Why am I taking your furniture? I—" Alyxander put his hand on his confused brother's shoulder and patted him.

"Okay, okay," Adonyjah interjected. "Everyone chill. Haze, this was supposed to be a surprise from all of us till this a-hole brothah of yours jacked it up."

"Adyson, the reason most ex-convicts are re-incarcerated is because they become frustrated with the system's inability to help them. For most, their families have nothing to do with them. At least seventy percent of the inmates, if not more, leave prison and are homeless until they commit another crime, returning them to the system," Alyxander said.

"When I was about to be released I had no idea where I was going; I was lost. I spent many sleepless nights worrying. I wondered how I could live so high on the hog, and then lose everything: my car, house, clothes, furniture, and most important, my drug contacts. So yeah, I was gonna start selling drugs again to get back on my feet.

"I didn't get many visits either, except Devon. So, I was pissed with everyone in our retarded family, havin' no intention of seeing them when I got out, was my plan. He shook his head, thinking back to that first day. I didn't get the homecoming you did, just Dev, Zave, Donny, and Stud. Still, I was overwhelmed to see them.

"They set me up in a nicely-furnished apartment equipped with everything I'd need; even a bike was in the foyer, dinner was waiting for me. It was my new home; wasn't what I was used to, but it was betta than the prospects of where I was goin': the shelter."

One by one they sat on the floor, listening to Alyxander emotionally reminiscing. "I felt like my life was designed and controlled by these guys." He threw his thumb in their direction. "I had a job, I was enrolled in school; I had to attend 'The Blind Leading the Blind' spiritual classes. and I...uhm..."

He was overwhelmed by his reflection; he stopped, staring down at his hands.

"Ya know," he continued, "I was pissed with them, resented them because I felt they were tryin' to control me. I just knew they thought they were better than me, and waiting for me to screw up. It was hard being where I was as a man, and havin' to have other men pull me up.

"One day I was so depressed, I visited ZaBryna after work. I tried to just sit and hang with her, but ya know how she is... we can't hide stuff from her. That maternal radar's always on." He smiled, reflecting.

"When she asked what was wrong, I didn't BS; I told her. She rubbed through my hair, twirling her fingers, massaging my scalp."

"Yeah, she always does that when we're upset," Adonyjah interjected.

Alyxander had crept into the depths of his memory. "I remember every single word my mother said. 'Alyxander, baby, step away from your ego and slaughter your pride, son, before they consume you. It's those two qualities that got you in trouble in the first place. You had to be rich, and have the most expensive gifts to shower your friends and women with. Where were they when you fell off your chariot? Did any of them, even one, visit you? No baby, they didn't.

"Your brothers wanna contribute to your future success. Honey, you gotta crawl before you can walk, because if you don't, you won't ever master the art of walking, or running without constantly stumbling. They're not controlling you; they've designed a path for you that won't lead back to jail. Their efforts don't make you less of a man; they make you a stronger man. Receiving the products of their efforts doesn't make you a weaker man, but a wiser one. Right now, you can't appreciate it because you think they're controlling you, but they've just intercepted your efforts to worship money, and material things.'"

Alyxander looked around disoriented, returning from his mental journey. "Woo, did I go on a trip?"

"I never knew you felt like that. We just wanted to help you get a fresh start," Adonyjah said.

"Donny, you all did; and I appreciate it. My reaction to you guys helping me was my issue, not yours."

"Adyson, I didn't mean to bypass my point; we wanna help you. I want you to experience the birth of a different life from what we've known." Alyxander sighed.

"I don't know what to say, but I can't take Zavian's furniture."

"We didn't know this clown was going to do this; everything

will be straightened out. I promise you that," Adonyjah said, shooting Zavian an annoyed look.

"Jeez, do you think I don't know what I'm doing? That furniture is for Adyson. I gave it to him because the mattress is comfortable. Look, when Alyxander came home, my money was tied up with this house, and so I couldn't financially help like I wanted. I wanna do this for Adyson."

"Hey, what's the time?" Alyxander asked, looking at his watch. "Crap, we've only got forty minutes to drop these things off at the house, and get back to ZaBryna's. Let's pray before we head back."

"Pray?" Adyson inquired.

"Yea, we started doing that last year," Adonyjah said.

"Devon, will you lead us in prayer?" Zavian asked.

They closed their eyes, and bowed their heads as Devon prayed. Adyson squinted his eyes, looking at each one, hoping to find someone else looking around too. Finally he closed his eyes and tried to listen again. Still he could only hear Devon mumbling. He opened his eyes, this time to see if anyone else was having the same difficulty as him.

Everyone seemed to understand him because they were nodding in agreement. He closed his eyes again to no avail, Devon was still mumbling. *I know one thing, I'll be glad when he finishes this praying thing; I'm hungry.* As he opened his eyes again, his brothers finalized their prayers.

"I'll call ZaBryna and let her know we're running late," Alyxander said, picking up his cell phone.

"We're really going to be late if we start moving this furniture now. Why don't we leave it until tomorrow?" Zavian suggested.

"Hey listen, y'all don't have to go through this. I have a list of shelters in the area; I was planning to stay there anyway," Adyson interjected.

"We gotta roll. Something's goin' on at the house," Alyxander interrupted.

"What?" Adonyjah asked, frustrated.

"Man, I don't know. Aryngton's stressing 'cause he's trying to calm the kids down; I can hear them screaming. Sounds like things are being thrown and ZaBryna's screaming. Only God knows what's happening."

"Where's Aryn in all of this?" Adonyjah asked as they were putting on their coats, walking towards the door.

"Shoot, who knows; heard the commotion, and told Aryngton we're on our way."

Rushing out the door and closing it, Zavian breezed by Marian walking up his driveway. "Happy New Year, Marian." The rest followed close behind, nodding as they passed her.

MARIAN SPUN AROUND TO WATCH THEM CLIMB SILENTLY INTO the Escalade. "Hey. Am I invisible?" She looked around, waiting to receive a response from somewhere. She looked back at the house in its darkness, and then back at the rear of the truck, already down the street.

ADYSON SAT IN THE FRONT PASSENGER SEAT, WRINGING HIS hands, staring out the window. *What could've happened?* He thought about Alyxander's conversation describing the scene he perceived over the phone and flashbacked to when they were kids. They would scatter into their rooms, closets, bathtubs, anywhere to ensure security. Now he envisioned his niece and nephews doing the same. He could feel the soreness in his jaw from his tightly clenched teeth. His heart was throbbing in his ears as he tried to envision the scene they were going to witness. *The only difference: Avery's wheelchair bound and we're adults.*

How can someone disrupt anything from a wheelchair? I'm a grown man feeling like I wanna jump out this vehicle and never look back. He shifted his eyes to look at Adonyjah driving; he was composed. *Look at him driving, and talking like we're still just going to Mom's house for dinner.* Finally he heard his own voice. "Donny, man, can you drop me off at the metro?"

"Where you going?" Alyxander asked, pulling up on his seat; looking at the side of his face.

"Uhmmmm, I think I'm just gonna take a ride and see if I can check out some shelters."

"You ain't stayin' in no shelter, man. We all got homes, and you think you're stayin' in a shelter? C'mon Haze, get real," Zavian said, impatiently.

"Look I'm not tryin' to be no burden. I-I-uh...look, shoot, I can't go to those people's house with all that chaos. Just drop me at the metro, Donny, please," Adyson begged this time.

"It's New Year's Eve, Haze, you ain't gonna find no crummy shelter," Alyxander shouted,

"What the crap is—"

"Okay, hold it," Adonyjah shouted. "We're all responding off what's goin' on at the house. E'rybody just calm down a minute."

"What's goin' on, Haze?"

"Nothin' man, I just ain't feelin' like I need to go to that house. I—"

"You don't have to. I'll drop you off at my house, but you ain't stayin' at no shelter. You can stay there until tomorrow. Okay?"

Silence loomed inside the vehicle for almost five minutes until

Adonyjah broke it. "Man, I didn't even get a chance to shower and change."

"Me either," all but Adyson chorused.

"Well, I don't think we all need to go over there. I'll go over, and y'all go home and change before dinner," Adonyjah said.

"If that's the case, Adyson can go home with me, shower and relax," Alyx suggested.

"That's okay; I really don't have anything to change into."

"Yeah you do. Your clothes are at your apartment," Devon said.

"We wanted it to be a surprise, but crap keeps happening." Adonyjah smiled at him.

"You're my freakin' roommate, dude," Alyx proudly announced, shaking Adyson's shoulders.

Adyson sat up, stunned. "What? I don't have no money to pay no rent. What's wrong with you all? I ain't got a job, nothin'. How—"

"We already know that," Devon interrupted him. "Calm down, man, it's not that serious. Donny and I pay the mortgage. Zavian shares a portion of the utilities and insurance on the place."

"So, I'm livin' with Alyx?" he responded sarcastically.

"No Haze, we're subleasing from them," Alyxander said, pointing to Adonyjah and Devon.

Adyson shook his head, "I can't. I just can't."

"You can't what?" Adonyjah snapped. "Lawd help us, now what's the problem? You're tellin' me you would rather sleep in a nasty, unkept, unsafe shelter than—"

"Donny, Donnnny, hold up man. Let's find out what's on his mind," Zavian suggested. "Haze, what's the problem, man? Are you havin' a problem with the arrangement?"

Adyson shook his head again, whispering his response. "No,

I... uh, it's just too much comin' at me, and I can't see what's before me. Suppose I mess up again, then what?"

"This arrangement isn't about you doing right or wrong, this is about you gettin' assistance with getting on your feet. If at some point you decide you don't wanna do anything better with your life, ya move out. But for now we thought ya needed assistance getting on your feet," Zavian explained.

"Alyx told you he was given the same opportunity. What you do with it is your business. No judgment, just like there was none for him. Each day you wake up, you make your own decisions for your life without any obstacles or distractions," Adonyjah said, calmly.

Adyson looked out the passenger window, sorting through all the information they'd given him. *Accepting their offer would make my life a lot easier. It'll give me an address for the Probation Man and make seeking employment easier. I could just stay in my room and stay outta everyone's way.*

Adonyjah pulled up at the corner of his parents' block. "Let me go see what's goin' on; I'll see you guys later." Alyx walked around the truck and got in the driver seat, catching the keys as Adonyjah threw them. Adyson watched his brothers' interaction, amazed at how all of them re-acted to one another without communication.

Even when Alyx called their parents and found there was a problem, they left the house, no words exchanged, no plans, no strategies. They just got into Adonyjah's truck. Now here again, Adonyjah got out the car and Alyx stepped in. All of them had some kind, of unspoken code.

"Zavian, are you goin' with Devon, or comin' with me and Haze?" Alyx asked, pulling up to Devon's house.

"I'm gonna hang with Haze and you; Devon's got some issues with Trazie that I ain't tryin' to deal with."

"What, makes you think I got issues with Trazie?" Devon asked, annoyed.

"Man, please. The only reason you've been with us all day is because you two are probably beefin'."

"Later for y—"

Zavian laughed, interrupting Devon's train of thought, causing Devon and Alyx to join in. Devon slammed the door and walked up the driveway, shaking his head.

Five minutes later they arrived at the newly renovated Phoenix Condominium. Alyx swiped his card to gain entry to the complex's parking lot. Adyson got out the car, slowly following Alyx and Zavian to the elevators that took them to the eleventh floor. Again, feelings of exclusion loomed over him, being the only one who didn't know where they were going. Stepping off the elevator, Alyx reached in his pants pocket, pulled out a key chain and handed it to Adyson. "Suite 1155, to the left of the elevator."

"Thanks, man," Adyson responded, heading left. He twirled the key around and in between his fingers as he walked towards the condo. Turning the key in the lock, he opened the door and stepped over the threshold of the place he would now call home. Alyx stepped in behind him and hit the switch on the wall. Adyson stood in the same spot he stepped in and looked around. The hallway walls were painted black, ceiling and baseboards were white. To the right of him was a wall full of hand-painted pictures.

A large portrait of their parents hung in the center. Slightly to the right above it was another hand-painted picture of Adonyjah, probably at about five years old. Underneath were two pictures: one of him and one of Adryanah. To the left of the parents' portrait was

Alyxander and underneath that was a picture of Aryngton and Aryn. The pictures formed the shape of a heart, surrounding ZaBryna's and Avery's pictures, with the portraits of Zayne, Sayvion, Symaya, and Zabryna completing the lower portion. Adyson stood staring in disbelief, using his finger to trace the faces of both his parents.

"Who drew this?" he asked, turning to look at Alyxander.

"I started drawing to pass the time when I was in prison. So when I moved in here, I decided to put them on the wall. It was kind of a healing journey for me." Adyson nodded, confirming he understood.

He turned around to look at the opposite wall. Alyxander had created a photo gallery that included pictures from their childhood and memories of special occasions. There were even pictures of himself and Adryanah when they were younger. Emotions viciously whirled around in his stomach, forcing him to walk away.

The kitchen was the first entrance they came to. "Anyone wanna beer?" Alyxander asked.

"Naw man, I want food," Zavian responded. Adyson remained quiet.

The kitchen carried the effect of a bachelor's existence: blue walls, dish rags and towels. He passed the doorway and immediately walked into the living room, where his favorite colors— beige and brown— were on display.

"Nice furniture," Adyson noted.

"Compliments of our brothers and Value City." Alyxander laughed. "They were kind enough to give us a large screen TV, a Wii and some games. There's a PlayStation in the cabinet under the television too," Alyxander said, excitedly.

Us? Adyson thought.

"Your room's back here." Alyxander pointed to the foyer leading to the bedrooms.

"I thought you only had a studio," Adyson stated.

"Yeah, I did when I first got home, but then when we found out your release date, Adonyjah bought this two-bedroom and den."

"There's a den too?" Adyson asked.

"Yeah, you wouldn't think these condos are as big as they are, but they're roomy. The den's Adryanah's when she gets out. You know, it keeps us from having to move again, and saves on expenses."

They stopped at the first door. "This is your room," Zavian said, pushing the door open. "I guess you'll be painting it when you get settled."

Adyson walked around the room with approval. A small desk was placed by the window with a computer and bubble-jet printer on top. He passed his hands across the desk, then he walked over and opened the door to the walk-in closet. Boxes were stacked on the floor, there was a black suit hanging on the rack and three dress shirts with matching ties: one white, a grey, and a red also hung there. He closed the door and stood in the middle of the floor, speechless.

"Wanna see my room?" Alyxander asked. "C'mon, your television and DVD player are in the den. We didn't know if you wanted it on the wall or if you'd want a TV stand. This is the master bedroom; I got my own bathroom, you have the hall bathroom. ZaBryna bought us new towel sets last week. Oh, the boxes in your closet are your clothes. You probably ain't gonna be thrilled with your threads, but it's just to get you started. I wasn't thrilled with my gear, that's for sure; but, it beats havin' nothin'."

Adyson nodded his head in agreement. "I really appreciate all of this."

"Haze, we'll move your furniture here tomorrow; in the meantime, you can sleep at my house tonight," Zavian offered.

Nodding his head was all Adyson could do.

❧ 9 ❧

SOME THINGS NEVER CHANGE

Adonyjah briskly walked down the street to his parents' condo. Stepping into the foyer, he could hear screaming. He stopped and leaned against the door.

Jesus help us! What in the world could anyone find to fight about on New Year's Eve? He couldn't conceive of starting another year with his family and the fighting. On the other hand, he knew he couldn't leave them to deal with this nightmare alone. *Gee, Breena and Aryn didn't even wanna go. Stupid Alyx and his bright ideas. I'm tired of telling him that we ain't a good family.*

"Some things never change," he yelled, grabbing his head with both hands. He could hear Aryn cursing; her level of rage frightened him. *Where does that rage come from? This girl always got her way.* He looked around as though he would hear the answer. The sound of his niece crying permeated the corridor; he was sure she could be heard by the tenants.

He walked to the door of the first-level and knocked, choosing not to use his keys. Within seconds the door flew open with a wide-eyed Zayne gripping the other side of the doorknob.

"What's up, neph?" was all Adonyjah thought to say to the terrified-looking child.

"Uncle Donnay!" Zayne yelled, climbing up his legs, into his arms, babbling, "Mommy's in the kitchen, with Beena and Av—"

"Let go of my neck. It's gonna be okay," he responded in a calm voice, standing Zayne on the floor.

"Mommy's real mad," he whispered, calmer.

"Don't worry, I'm here. Go get your coat and shoes."

"Happy New Year's!" Adonyjah yelled, walking down the foyer to the terrified screams of Symaya in the living room. Aryngton was holding Symaya and Sayvion on his lap. Sayvion's face was buried in his uncle's armpit; Symaya screamed and trembled. The brothers shook their heads, acknowledging that they understood the children's plight. Adonyjah calmly walked back to the hall closet and took out the twins' outer garments.

"Zayne, son, can you get their shoes, please?"

"Okay," he replied, running back down the hall.

"Uncle Stud's gonna take you guys out."

A look of relief whirled across Zayne's face as he handed Adonyjah the shoes. Adonyjah turned to Aryngton, lifted Symaya off his lap, handing him Sayvion's outer garments and shoes. Sitting Symaya down on his lap, he put on her shoes and coat. He and Aryngton finished at the same time and stood up, walking towards the front door.

"King Aryngton Stud, will take you guys out, and I shall make your castle safe again," he said, kissing each one on their forehead. Symaya looked at her uncle with loving eyes and a weak smile as he placed her back in Aryngton's arms; within seconds they were gone.

Adonyjah closed the door and leaned on it; walking into the kitchen, he yelled, "H-e-l-l-o-oo."

ZaBryna rushed from the corner and wrapped her arms around her eldest son's waist, hugged him, and tiptoed to kiss him on his cheek. "Hey, I didn't hear you come in," she said, nervously.

"How can you hear anything with all the scream—"

"Don't start, Donny!" Aryn interrupted. "I know that punk, Stud called you. He's like a little gurl, always running after you to protect his dumb butt."

Adonyjah scanned the room to find Paul squeezed up in the corner by the freezer. Aryn was standing over her father with a frying pan in her hand. Avery was slumped in his wheelchair, blood dripping from his lips, and the side of his head. He never thought he would ever feel such despair for his father. Yet there he stood in the doorway of his parents' kitchen, feeling his heart torn apart at the hands of his baby sister. "What's going on?" he asked, his voice struggling to remain calm. "Why's Avery bleeding, Aryn?"

"This Motherf—"

"Aryn!" he interrupted, raising his hand, "Without the profanity."

"We get home, and Paul had Avery in the back cleanin' him up or whateva. Breena and I started to get the table set before warming the food. Naw, straight to the point, look around you; ev'rything you see on this floor's what he threw at my mother." The tears streamed down Aryn's face. She opened her arms, and waved them around the kitchen, never letting go of the frying pan.

"Look Donny, this is what this moron thinks of our mother after all she's done for him; after all the years she's loved him, been loyal to him and respected him."

"Adonyjah. Adonyjah." ZaBryna shouted his name, afraid of what her son would do. "Please don't call Alyxander."

Adonyjah gently moved his mother away from him, and slowly walked to the other side of the table that was in the middle of the kitchen. His mouth hung open. Broken plates, cups, and cooking utensils were on the floor. The pan of cornbread, yams and potato salad dressed the floor. The lower cupboards had something red smeared across them; it looked like blood. Then he saw the ketchup bottle several feet away, with the cap split. Like an eagle, he gracefully spread his arms open, turning slowly around the room to absorb the whole picture.

He stopped, and lowering his arms looked at his mother. Terror filled her eyes and the very core of her being was trembling. "Are you hurt?" Adonyjah asked, in a low, controlled voice.

"Adonyjah please, everything's alright," ZaBryna begged.

"Are you hurt?" he asked again; this time his voice was more demanding.

"Adonyjah, it's okay, baby. It's New Year's Eve."

"Mother. Are you hurt?" His voice was firm and demanding.

She turned her back to him, wincing from the pain as she pulled apart her waist-long hair to show the gash in the back of her head. A burgundy bruise covered the upper area of her right arm, disappearing under her sleeve.

Donny turned away from his mother and looked at Aryn. Her eyes no longer showed the rage they had earlier; she was too scared to hold on to her anger. He then turned his attention to Paul. "What happened, Mr. Santana?"

"Uh, uhm... sir, I was getting Mr. Clark dressed for this evening's dinner. That's what your brother, Mr. Alyxander had requested I—"

Adonyjah nodded his head impatiently, encouraging him to continue.

"Uhm, Mr. Clark heard your mother come in. He asked me, uh, uh... what time it was and I told him. He seemed anxious, but I didn't pay it much mind. While I was cleaning his bathroom, he said he wanted to get a snack; so I wheeled him out here. Mrs. uh... Clark was putting something in the lower freezer." His voice escalated as he tried to get some understanding of his story. "I saw him raise his arm, and bring it down in her direction; I heard her scream and she grabbed her head," Paul finalized, shaking his head from side to side.

"Mr. Clark, I never expected this; I don't even know where that stick came from. I, uh, I'm sorry. I wouldn't have brought him out here had I known he would do this. I never thought he'd hurt his own wi—" Adonyjah raised his hand, interrupting Paul.

There's no blame to be placed, he wasn't hired to be a bodyguard for ZaBryna. Shoot, I didn't know he could do this much damage and I've been around the last three years. I wonder if Avery always knew he had that much strength.

"Donny?" Aryn interrupted his thoughts. "You okay?"

He walked over to his mother and sat her in the chair facing the front door, so he could get a better look at her head.

"Aryn, get me the peroxide."

"Donny, you okay?" Aryn asked, concerned with her brother's calmness.

"Get me the peroxide, please," Adonyjah repeated.

Aryn looked at Paul. He shrugged his shoulders, then she left to go get the peroxide.

"Here, Donny." She handed him the gauze and peroxide. She walked over to the kitchen sink and grabbed some paper towels and handed them to ZaBryna to wipe the tears that continuously flowed down her face.

"Paul, do you think she needs stitches?" Adonyjah asked.

"I'm just an aide, sir."

"I know, but I'm just asking if you think she needs stitches from looking at it?"

"Well, I think she should see a doctor to make sure there's no concussion or stitches needed."

"Who needs stitches?" Alyxander asked, walking around Adonyjah to see who was sitting in the chair.

"Somebody help us," ZaBryna screamed in anguish.

"What happened to her?" Alyx yelled, looking at Aryn. She stood in front of Avery in a protective stance.

"Ah crap," Adonyjah yelled. "Paul, help my mother, please." He handed him the gauze and shifted his position to get in front of Alyxander, resting his palms on his chest. "Now you listen to me, Alyx, don't take off. Where's Adyson?"

"I'm right here," Adyson answered, sounding in a much better mood than earlier. He turned and walked around Paul extending his hand toward him. "Hey, I'm Ad...*a*—what the..." He stopped and looked down at ZaBryna crying silently, then shot his eyes over to Aryn's tear-stained face and then down to his father, sitting in the wheelchair. Bewildered, he completely stepped around Paul and stood next to Alyxander. Donny placed his right palm on Adyson's chest. "Listen, you two," he said cautiously, "things are bad enough and the children will be back here soon. Where's Zavian and Devon?"

"Parking," Adyson responded. His eyes still absently focused on Paul holding the peroxide to ZaBryna's head.

Alyxander mumbled something inaudible, his wide hazel eyes stayed fixed on Avery's lowered head.

"Oh God, please. Let's everybody stay calm," Adonyjah begged. "Alyx, call the ambulance, please."

"Did he"–Alyxander pointed at Avery—"do this to her?"

"I'm sorry," Avery said. It was the first time they had ever heard him apologize.

"You're sorry?" Alyxander repeated, slowly. What exactly, are you sa—"

He tried to step around from Adonyjah's arm. "Wait a minute, Alyx," Adonyjah shouted, fear and anxiousness piercing his words. "Everybody needs to stay calm, doggone it," Adonyjah demanded.

"Got us some champagne to bring in the new—" Devon stopped, causing Zavian to walk into the back of him. Devon walked over to Adonyjah and stood in front of Alyxander.

"Aryngton's walking up the block with the kids," Zavian informed Adonyjah.

"Stud, ain't nothing but a pun—"

"Aryn, shut up."

"Donny, you not gonna keep talkin' to me like that!"

"Could you handle those three kids this long under these circumstances alone? Huh?"

She dropped her head, whispering, "No."

"Then we all do what we do best and his ain't dealing with this crappy confusion. Shoot, *I* don't wanna be here, if truth be told." Adonyjah moved his arm off Adyson, who was still standing silently in the same position. He reached in his pocket and pulled out a hundred-dollar bill. "Zay, give Stud the keys to the truck and this. Tell him to take them somewhere to eat. They shouldn't have to be exposed to any more of this. Matter-of-fact, you go with him."

"Naw man, you might need me here," Zavian challenged, concerned for what might happen. He started thinking of all the times he had heard Adonyjah and Alyxander vow they'd kill their father if he ever touched their mother again.

"I'm good," Alyx said, assuring Zavian he could leave. "I just wanna know what this fool's sorry for."

"I'm gonna call an ambulance," Zavian announced.

"Excuse me, Mr. Clark, your mother's shirt is saturated. Seems like this thing's bleeding worse than we thought," Paul said.

"The ambulance is on its way," Zavian shouted, walking out the door.

Adyson stooped down in front his mother. "Adyson, please, not now!" Adonyjah warned.

He pushed back her hair to look at her face, shaking his head from side to side. He got on his knees, kissing her tears, before wiping them, with the paper towel she held in her hand. "It's gonna be alright," he assured behind his sobbing. He rested his head on ZaBryna's lap, kissing her hand, which lay next to him. Adonyjah, Alexander, Aryn and Devon stared in disbelief; it was the first time in life Adyson had consoled his mother. Adonyjah began picking up the broken dishes. Alyxander assured Devon he was okay and then joined his brother in the cleanup. Aryn picked up the dishcloth, wiping off the residue from the condiments plastered on the cupboards.

Avery sat quietly watching the cleanup, hoping they'd forget he was there. *I should've just waited until everyone was gone; I don't know what I was thinking. These blasted kids think that whore's an angel. Normally, she'd have made excuses to keep them out of here. Trick, just gonna leave me to go out. I'm gonna git her good tonight.*

"This way, please," Zavian directed the EMS workers to ZaBryna.

"I thought you left," Adonyjah said.

"We decided to wait until the ambulance came."

"The kids saw the ambulance?" Adonyjah and Alyxander shouted together.

"No, they're around the corner, singing songs with Aryngton. I'm goin' now to meet them. Let us know what's happening."

"We'll call y'all when we know something," Alyxander responded.

"Sir, can you please stand up so we can assess the patient." Adyson lifted his head and stood up.

"Hey, she ain't the only one hurt in here. Look at my head too," Avery yelled.

"Oh, you got hurt, Avery?" Adyson said, racing over, dragging Avery out of the wheelchair and slamming him against the refrigerator. "How did you get hur—"

Alyxander, Adonyjah and Devon ran to where he was. Devon attempted to grab Avery from Adyson's hands. Adonyjah wedged himself between the two of them and Alyxander grabbed Adyson from the back, tussling until he released their father.

"Git off me, fool. I want him to fight me like he did her," Adyson screamed hysterically.

"This is the man that taught me how to treat a woman. This is the man that trained me to think women should be beaten into submission. Tell them, Avery, 'Women don't know what they want, you gotta make them do what you want. They'll just tell you 'no' to mess with you.

"'Women don't love you, unless you beat 'em. Look at your mother, why you think she love me? It's 'cause I whip her butt.' I've listened to that since I was three years old."

Aryn was on the floor at Adyson's feet, sobbing. She could remember those conversations her father would have with him every time he beat up their mother.

"Why you all protecting him? Look at her, Donny."

"We're not protecting him, Adyson, it's you we're protecting. He ain't worth you goin' back to prison."

"I didn't rape her. She liked me; we both liked each other. We just hugged, kissed and... She changed her mind. You turned off the lights. When I spoke to him," Adyson pointed at Avery, "he said 'take it, she wants it rough'." He dropped to the floor, sobbing hysterically. "Why did I listen to him about my mother? You told me take it; it's owed to me." Adyson was on the floor gasping for air, "You said if I didn't demand what was mine... But I didn't. I didn't."

Alyxander slid to the floor next to him and held him. "He lied to me. He said, 'plead guilty; it's a first offense'." Adonyjah flung his head around to look at Adyson, and then at his father.

The paramedics took ZaBryna out on the stretcher as they exited the front door, then two more ambulances arrived with two squad cars. Paul directed the paramedics to the corner where Avery was; the second group moved in to help Adyson. They had to pry Adyson from Alyxander; his brother was clutched to his chest, tears streaming down his face.

"What happened here?" one of the officers asked Adonyjah, holding his pen to his report.

"That fool was born," Adonyjah shouted, pointing to Avery. "Get him outta here before I have to go to jail, pleaaaaaaase."

"Aryn, let me talk to you," Avery cried, extending his hands towards his daughter. "I'm sorry, baby girl."

"Get him out," Alyxander yelled, still holding the oxygen mask to Adyson's face.

"I'm fine," Adyson said, pushing the mask away.

Adonyjah stood next to the paramedic, giving him the personal information and ensuring the bill for Adyson was sent to him. "Thank you, and Happy New Year's," he said as they were leaving with the empty stretcher.

"Mr. Clark, will Mrs. Clark be pressing charges?" Officer Rogers asked.

"Yes," Alyxander intervened. "He opened up the back of her head."

"Wait a minute, Alyx," Adonyjah countered.

"No Donny, enough's enough."

"But when ZaBryna gets out, she gonna drop the charges," Adonyjah argued.

"Not necessarily," said Officer Stephenson, shooting his eyes at Rogers for allowing them to think they had a choice. "Any kind of domestic violence changes things."

"Well good," said Alyx, "because this is too much."

When Adonyjah returned to the kitchen, he found Aryn on her knees, her arms wrapped around Adyson's neck. Alyxander and Devon were leaning against the sink with their arms folded, staring at them. He picked up the bowl of potato salad, covered it, and placed it on the table. He picked up the rest of the food, stacking the bowls on the table. Alyx and Devon eventually joined in to help. And then Aryn and Adyson joined them. The tears continued to stream down Adyson's face. He couldn't imagine how he would ever face his siblings again.

"I think we should finish cleaning later. Let's go to the hospital to check on ZaBryna," Adonyjah suggested when the food was put away. "Or I can go and you all can relax and eat."

"I'm goin' with you," was the consensus, making him very happy. For the first time in his life, he didn't want to be alone. He never thought he'd ever need any of his siblings, because he was the one always needed; however, tonight was different.

"Donny man, thanks," said Adyson, "for everything you're

trying to do. Uhm, but I think I should pass up your offer to help me. Uh... there's just some things, I mean there's a lot of things I need to sort out. You know what I'm saying? I mean, my life's a total mess."

Adonyjah put his arms around his brother's shoulder. "This isn't the time to make any decisions, Haze. Not tonight... you can't make life-decisions after what we just went through. We need each other if we're going to ever recover from our pasts; we're gonna have to hold on to one another, and more importantly, hold on to God."

"It took Alyx and Stud to make me understand that. We need one another because we're all a mess; but, we can recover. Some of us are weak, where others are strong. We need to draw on each other's strength to get past our individual weaknesses. After all, division hasn't done this family any good, has it?" They all shook their heads no.

Aryn walked over to Adonyjah, "I guess I owe my twin an apology, huh?"

He placed his arm on her shoulder. "Yeah... well, I owe all of you an apology for not stepping up and making us a team."

"Hold it," Alyxander interjected, "we're not going to start holding on to blame, wasting our valuable time together apologizing. We did the best we could with what we had. Now we're moving on to a betta future."

"Group hug," Devon said. "This is too much drama. You Clarks breed so much drama."

"Shut up, Devon!" Alyxander said, pretending to wrestle him.

"Excuse me, Mr. Clark?"

"Paul, I didn't know you were still here," said Adonyjah.

"Did you want me to remain with your father?"

"Uh no, he's fine," Adonyjah replied.

"I wanna apologize for that incident; I didn't know—"

"No, *I'm* sorry. We didn't know he had mobility. He's been in that wheelchair for three years, depending solely on our mother. Who would've thought he had strength in his arms," Alyxander responded.

❧ 10 ❧

THE GUEST

"Ma...Poppasan, we're here," Ayden Smith shouted. "Where's everyone?"

"Gremmier and Poppasan went out."

"Can I watch TV?" five-year-old Keith asked.

Keith Smith put on his pants and ran down the steps. "Boy, TV's more important than looking for your Poppa?" he asked, stretching his arms out to catch his grandchildren.

"Hey son, where's Sharon and the girls?"

"Kaycee and Cody fought all the way here, so Sharon's schooling them."

"Where's Mom?" Ayden asked, surprised that Rita hadn't come to greet them.

"In the kitchen," Keith replied smugly. Ayden shot his father a suspicious eye. "You okay?"

"Sure am. We're about to embark on a new year. I'm intending to embrace the arrival with a positive attitude."

"Sharon and I were talking about that this morning. She's

totally stressed about being laid off; She's not sleeping well and she's gained weight."

"Are you two okay?" Keith asked.

"Sure Pop, the one thing we'll always be is alright 'cause when I'm weak, she carries the faith banner for both of us. Now it's my time to hold that banner, but I hate seeing her so down."

"How are things with you and Ma?"

"I don't know, she's always angry and it's getting worse. I told her we're gonna have to talk, because we can't continue like this."

Ayden put his arms around his father and pulled him towards him. "It's gonna be alright. Maybe we should take her to see a doctor. It could be that menopause thing. They say it makes some women moody."

"Ayden, she's not moody... she's argumentative and rude and I'm sick of it. I leave work with all that craziness, and walk into Beirut when I get home—"

"Poppasan," Sharon sang, "how's my favorite father-in-law?"

"Doing great, now that my favorite and most beautiful daughter-in-law is here."

"Where's my boots?" Ayden laughed, referring to his over-the-top reference to Sharon. He took his wife's hand. "The kids still alive?"

"Sure, they are. I tied them up in the trunk. Naw, they're coming."

"Y'all need to watch this child." Rita stormed in the room dragging three-year-old Tiara behind her. "I'm tryna cook and she's wandering in my kitchen, touching everything and asking one question after another. I can't hear myself think."

"Honey, she wants to spend time with her gremmie," Keith responded patiently.

"Well that's why God gave children two grandpar—"

"Hello Mother, how are you?" Ayden intervened, kissing her on her cheek.

"Can I help you with anything?" Sharon asked, trying to suppress her anger.

"Sure, watch your kids; that's the only help I need!"

"Mother!" Ayden scolded, "The kids have been excited about visiting you and this is how you act?"

"How am I acting, Ayden? Your wife asked if she can help. I told her what I need."

"Let's go," Ayden snapped, taking Tiara out of Sharon's hands.

"Son wait, don't leave. Your mother's under a lot of pressure."

"Pressure? Pops, please. She has no children or financial responsibility. What's stressing her?"

"Ayden, your sisters will be disappointed," Sharon interjected.

"We'll see them another time."

"Daddy, please," little Keith cried, "can I stay?"

"Let's go, peewee."

He ran up to his grandfather and hugged him. It's okay, I'll come over soon," Keith said, comforting him. "What about the girls?"

"We'll pick them up from the store," Ayden answered.

"Ayden, please," Keith begged. "It's New Year's Eve."

"You think she's been like this the last few years; but, she's been this way our whole life. You're just reaping her venom now because you're alone with her," Ayden said, walking out the door.

"I'm sorry, Sharon." Keith hugged her. When they walked out the door, Ayden was sitting in the car watching his children walk up the street.

"Say bye to Poppasan, you two," he instructed.

"We're leaving? It was Gremmie, I bet," accused Cody.

"Stay in a child's place," Sharon scolded.

"C'mon over here and give your ole gramps a hug," Keith said, fighting back the tears. "I'm gonna see you all soon."

⊗⊰⊗

"WOMAN, WHAT IN THE WORLD IS YOUR PROBLEM?" KEITH yelled, before he reached the kitchen.

"Don't use that tone with me, Keith."

"Rita, you need to see a doctor. There have to be health issues affecting the way you act. Those children drove hours and you chased them away. Honey, I think we need to find out what's wrong."

"There's nothing wrong with me. Every holiday you seem to need this house occupied with the kids. Then they bring their friends and their children, so I'm in the kitchen all day and night. I'm sick of it!"

"Woman, they're *our* children. It's not like we see them often. This is the only time everyone gets together. You wouldn't have to do as much if you'd let us help. Sharon offered."

"What Sharon needs to do is focus on controlling that brat; she's always talkin'."

"That brat's our granddaughter. You're losing your mind."

"There ain't nothin' wrong with me; I just want to be left alone."

"By me?"

"By everyone!" she screamed.

Keith watched her carry on her task, humming as if nothing cross was said, then he left and went to the family room. He stared at the ceiling, searching for the answer to what had gone wrong in their relationship.

He had proposed marriage to Rita numerous times in the

thirty-three years they had shared. Each time she said no.

They'd started dating when she was sixteen; however, he had been speaking to her since the second week of her freshman year in high school. He knew the first day he saw her, she would be his wife. For her high school graduation, he asked her to marry him. She said they were too young.

She became pregnant with Arjasyah, terminating her enrollment the second semester in college. Keith smiled, as he remembered how excited he was about becoming a daddy. He'd just obtained his pilot's license, and was embarking on his second month after opening A-1 Courier Services.

He embraced the pregnancy, knowing it would work out well. He took on a night job delivering for a local pizza parlor, which helped keep them afloat. When Rita reached her eighth month, he asked her to marry him. Again, she said no.

Thinking back on the Lamaze classes, Keith smiled. He had thought it was his favorite, most rewarding experience in the whole having-a-baby thing. He loved having her lean back on his chest like she couldn't complete the birthing task without his coaching.

Lamaze was his favorite thing, until that day God blessed him with his gift; Arjasyah Marjae Smith. She was beautiful. She had light-bluish eyes and a round, beautifully shaped bald head, with evidence of reddish-brown hair hidden under her scalp. She had nothing that resembled Rita or him, not even her complexion. She was her own little pink-looking person.

He remembered that day, twenty-nine years ago like it was yesterday. He had panicked during Lamaze, imagining himself passing out when he had to cut the umbilical cord. He didn't. He took those scissors, freeing his gorgeous princess from her lifeline.

Arjasyah had changed his attitude towards success, even the way he saw Rita.

The woman had endured a pain no man would ever know, to bring forth life. She'd unselfishly allowed her body to be battered to show the world their product of love. He fell in love with her again; she would eternally be his queen.

He leaned over as she lay exhausted, and asked her to be his wife. She said no. Keith closed his eyes, trying to fall asleep but he couldn't. It always bothered him that she wouldn't marry him.

Two years later, Rita became pregnant again. God would bless him with his son; he was sure. Arjasyah would always be his princess, but his son would carry his name. The second pregnancy seemed to be a little more strenuous on Rita, so he hired a nanny to take care of Arjasyah, cook and clean. By the seventh month Rita was huge; she was confined to the bed.

Keith was at every doctor's appointment. By thirty-four weeks, Dr. Solomon induced labor. Keith was terrified but was assured that it was the best thing for Rita.

The night before the scheduled birth, he held Rita in his arms. So many emotions flooded him; he remembered wondering what Rita felt. Before she dozed off, he proposed again. She rejected him. He didn't think she could hurt him any deeper until she told him the baby's name would be Ayden Smith. She claimed it had always been her desire to name her son Ayden. He smiled at how much he spoiled her.

Ayden weighed in at four pounds, six ounces, a mere two minutes before his secret four pound, five ounce companion, Adyna. By the time Alyssia was born three years later, Keith gave up hope on marriage.

"Keith, telephone," Rita snarled, shoving the phone in his chest.

"Hey Poppasan, did I wake you?" Arjasyah asked in her baby voice.

"No, Princess." He rubbed his forehead. "What's wrong?"

'Nothin', uh... we just left the airport. I was wondering if Parris can invite her cousin to dinner."

"Did you ask your mother?" Keith inquired.

"Nnnnoooo, I'm asking you." Arjasyah laughed.

"You're a spoiled woman. You knew I wasn't going to say no to you. You should've asked your mother, though; she's the cook."

"We'll bring extra desserts. Is that okay?"

"Princess, you don't have to do that. Tell Parris any family of hers, is ours."

"Thanks, Pop. Lovin' ya always."

"Lovin' you back, baby."

৩২৩

Sharon turned to check on the sleeping children, annoyed with Ayden for allowing his mother to work him. *Rita's an unhappy, wicked woman. I always expect the worst from her and she never disappoints me. If it wasn't for Poppasan, I'd never visit, but I've been blessed with the best father-in-law.* She understood why Alyssia left home at sixteen and never returned. *The poor child got the worst deal out of all the Smith children. Rita seemed to hate her for being born. She acted like Alyssia got her pregnant.*

"So, you going to continue ignoring me?" Ayden asked Sharon, reaching over to hold her hand. Sharon kept her eyes closed to avoid talking.

"Let's stay in a hotel in Atlantic City so the kids can feel like they went somewhere New Year's Eve. We could go to the pool; plus, I'll stay with the kids so you can go to the casino. Shar, I know you hear me. You know we don't ignore one another, please don't give my mom power."

"Oh, trust me, your mama has no power over me. AC, how could you allow her to push your buttons, like that? I'm not angry because we left. I'm disappointed because you allowed your mother to hurt our children, taking them from their family."

"Babe, I'm not goin' to allow her to talk to you or Tiara like that," he refuted.

"She's my baby too, but she and Lil Keith cried themselves to sleep because they wanted Poppasan. And your dad, babe, you disappointed him. You know he gets crazy when all of us come home, pulling out all his toys and electronic games. It's bad enough we don't get to see the family often," Sharon continued. "It's just not right."

"You wanna go back?"

"Ayden, we're in Delaware."

"I don't care... we'll get off the next exit. C'mon babe, I just got caught up with my mother's nonsense. I didn't look at the whole picture. I'm sorry. Look, the kids are asleep; by the time we get back, they'll just be getting up."

⚘

"It's almost five o'clock; I'll set the table so when the kids get here we can eat," Keith offered, attempting to bring some peace to their home. "Oh uh, by the way, Princess asked if Parris can bring her cousin. I told her it's fine."

Rita slammed the knife she was holding on the counter. "I knew when she called you it was some crap like that."

"Rita, honey, it'll be fine."

"No, it won't, Keith. You know why? I'll tell you why. You

never tell those kids no. And you don't ask me before making decisions. I thought after they grew up and moved out, that would change, but it hasn't. We don't need any more blasted kids in this house. Arjasyah has five, Adyna has three and Ayden, four. Everywhere the three of them are, there's Parris and her, what... three children?"

"Ah no... four; she had another baby." He laughed.

"So, you think that's funny, huh? Now you got her cousin coming. I'm sick and tired of feeding all these people."

"Stop!" Keith shouted. "Sharon and Ayden wanted everyone at their new house for the holidays, but you refused to go; so, it was kept here. Now you're complaining about them coming here? For God's sake, these are our children, our grandchildren; we're a family. What's wrong with you?"

"Oh, so now Parris is our child too? I don't remember giving birth to her."

"Don't you dare start on Parris. When you had Ayden and Adyna, it was Connie who took care of Arjasyah for a month-and-a-half, so we could visit them. When we brought them home, she stayed with you while I worked; cooking, cleaning, taking care of Parris, Princess and the twins. That woman did it for seven months while you suffered with postpartum depression. She wouldn't take a dime from me. And we're not going to even touch the year-and-a-half she took care of those children when Alyssia was born. She was your friend. Yet, when she was diagnosed with cancer, you didn't extend a hand. That's why I was honored to take custody of Parris, when Connie passed."

"Well she wouldn't have had to keep Arjasyah, if you hadn't insisted that we visit those twins, every freakin' evening," Rita lashed back.

Keith grabbed her arm, pulling her to him; he lowered his

voice almost to a whisper. "Woman, you're not going to mess this day up for our kids. You're not chasing another one away; Alyssia and Ayden—" The doorbell rang.

Keith walked down the hall, his hands trembling with rage. It was the first time in all their years together, he felt like he could hit her. *How dare she talk about our kids like that?* He stopped to compose himself before opening the door. "Who goes there?" Keith teased.

"Poppasan, open the door!" five-year-old Gyara screamed.

He unlocked the door and hid in the family room behind the couch.

Gyara led the crew running to the family room. "Where is he?" she asked.

"He's behind the curtain," eight-year-old Isaiah shouted.

"Naw, he's behind this sofa," ten-year-old Derrick laughed.

Keith jumped out and popped his grandson in the head. "You just know everything, don't you?"

"I try."

"Hey, where's the rest of my grands?"

"I'm right here, Poppasan," chimed Jasyah.

"Lil girl, where's the rest of your clothes?"

"Pops, please. I'll be fifteen tomorrow."

"Yeah, well while you're here, you're gonna cover yourself; so, go change."

Jasyah pulled up the handle on her suitcase and leaned on it, staring at her grandfather.

"I know you're not surprised, JoJo. I told you Poppasan wasn't gonna allow that hootchie-momma outfit," Kennedy barged in. "That's why I wore pants. Like it, Pops?" She spun around showing off her slender, five-foot-eight physique.

"Jasyah, go up and change *now!*" he demanded, "and you

stop be—"

"I got a boyfriend. Did Mom tell you?" Kennedy asked.

"No! and I'm not sure I want to know. You're almost sixteen; in another year you'll start college. Don't let none of these boys get your head twisted. Your momma put you on birth control, yet? We don't do knock-ups here, okay?"

"Mama said you were blunt when it came to sex but dang, P—"

"Poppasan," sang Adyna and Arjasyah, both embracing their father.

"My Candy and Princess, I'm so glad to see my girls. Where's Parris, she changed her mind?"

"No, she went to pick up her cousin," Arjasyah responded.

"Poppasan," Xavier forced a deep voice.

"C'mon here, boy." Keith reached up, pulling him into a head-lock, "I swear I don't know why you people are so tall; but I can still knock ya out."

"Hey, Poppasan." Pleasure walked in carrying a baby wrapped in a blanket.

"Lawd, Pleasure, please tell me that ain't yours, 'cause I'm gonna have to get my belt."

"Ewww Poppa, I'm only thirteen. Dis Auntie Parris' baby, Karrington. She four months."

"Where's Kingston and Kareem? They went with her?" Keith inquired.

"Naw, they're playing basketball outside," Pleasure replied.

Keith sat in the recliner and took the baby from Pleasure. He looked in admiration at his family. *This is life, living long enough to watch your children grow up, blessing you with grandchildren.* He thought about his mother. She never got to meet her grandchildren. *She would've loved them.* He looked down at Karrington and thought about Connie, how unfortunate that she'd lost her battle when Parris was seven.

But he was blessed with sixteen grandchildren. The girls had married well; decent, strong, responsible men, with family values and integrity. Unfortunately, Adyna's husband, Bennett Marshall was killed in Iraq, two years earlier. He never allowed himself to think about Alyssia; he believed one day God would bless him to find her and her children.

He began bouncing little Karrington on his lap as he thought about Ayden. He'd done the best he could to teach Ayden, by example, how to be a man, father and husband. He and Sharon had a strong relationship. She was a good woman. His only thorn in life was Rita.

"Pops, you okay?" Adyna tapped him on his shoulder.

"Just admiring my beautiful family. I'm blessed."

"Where's Ayden?" Arjasyah asked.

'Uhm, they went back home," Keith whispered.

"What?" Adyna shouted, "What happened?"

"It's nothing, they'll be back—"

"No, wait a minute... where's Mother?" Adyna interrupted.

"Candy, please, don't start your mother up. She's having a rough time. These kids don't—"

"Uh-uhn, she and I need to talk!"

"Candy," Arjasyah said, "let it go, you know how she is. Let's just make the best of tonight; we can go to Jersey for a few days. Wanna go, Pops?"

"Yeah baby, that would be great. Candy, you alright with that?"

"She makes me sick," Adyna ranted, without answering her father. "That's her son, for God's sake; why would she allow them to drive all the way here, only for them to turn around and go right back."

He wanted to comfort Adyna, knowing her angst also came from the fact that they were inseparable as children so that when Ayden's company moved to Jersey a year ago, she became depressed. She'd lost not only her brother but her best friend, his wife.

❦

"WHAT'S TAKING PARRIS SO LONG?" ADYNA ASKED, PICKING UP her cell phone. "Parris?"

"Open the door, big head. Happy New Year's, Pops," Parris sang.

"You hiding my baby from me? She's gorgeous just like her mama. Where are my sons-in-law?"

"Kingston and Randal are at the bowling alley; you know how those two are. They begged for one game before dinner," Parris explained.

"And they didn't invite me, 'cause they were scared," Keith challenged. Kingston, Randal, Bennett and Sharon, grew up with the Smith children. When they were kids, Keith took them bowling on Saturdays. Although the girls loved their Saturday outings; the boys, being competitive, never lost their obsession for the game.

"This is my cousin, Marian and her daughters, Linda, Cynthia, and Jacinta." Parris introduced them to the group.

"I'm five," Linda interjected, showing five fingers.

"Thanks for having me. Parris told me so much about you and it's a pleasure to meet all of you," Marian said, giving a fake grin.

"Grab a seat, Marian. The girls can sit at the table with the other children," Keith instructed.

Parris pulled out a chair next to Keith and Marian slid into it.

Her movement did not go unnoticed by Rita who sat at the opposite end of the table.

"Marian, why don't you fix your daughters' plates," Arjasyah suggested. "That way—"

"Oh cuz, you can make their plates since you're standing," Marian interrupted, flagging her hand at Arjasyah. Parris took the plates from Arjasyah, and then led Cynthia and Linda to sit at the table. When she returned Adyna stood up, took the plates from Parris and handed them to Marian. "Make your children's plates."

Marian looked at Keith as though she expected him to say something in her defense before doing as she was told.

"Where do you work?" Rita asked.

"I'm a stay-at-home mom," Marian replied, with an air.

"What does your husband do for a living?" Rita continued to pry.

"I, uhm, I'm not married," Marian answered, shifting in her seat.

"So, you're on public assistance?" Rita was determined to insult Marian for trying to jostle her man. She was jealous but didn't know why. The tension in the room was so intense, that when the doorbell rang, Adyna was relieved for the diversion.

"Excuse me, sir, may I use your phone please?" Sharon asked, sneaking up behind Keith to hug him.

"Guurlll, you's a sight for sore eyes."

"Faaamillllllly," Ayden, Kingston and Randal shouted.

"Kingston, who won?" Keith always instigated between the men.

"Pops, I ain't tryin to embarrass a brothah so I'll tell you later," Kingston replied.

"Kingston lost." The women laughed.

11

WE ARE ONE

"We're leaving the hospital now; where are you guys?"

Aryngton yawned. "We're at Zavian's house. How's Bree?"

"She's got a concussion; plus it took twenty-eight stitches to close that thing. She's not talkin', just crying. The doctor says it's a combination of depression and anxiety or whatever. Stud, did you know he was beating her?"

"No. I didn't even know he had upper-mobility; she always had to do everything. He couldn't even hold his toothbrush. I would've told ya had I even *thought* he was doin' that. I wondered why she was still so afraid of him. I just thought she was avoiding his verbal abuse."

"Whoo, let's give this conversation a break. It's New Year's morning; we've gotta salvage what's left of it." Adonyjah forced a laugh. "We'll meet you at Zavian's and bring breakfast; tell him he's gonna use that dining room today."

"Will do. Uh, Donny, how's Adyson? I didn't have time to talk to him since he got home. I hope he didn't thrash Breena; you know how he is about his father."

"He's fine," Adonyjah responded, looking at Adyson with pride. "Stud, our family's gonna be alright." *Someone must've been prayin for us.*

෯

"UNCA DONNY'S HERE," ZAYNE SHOUTED.

"That's all you see?" Aryn teased.

"Is Breena okay?" Zayne asked.

"She's doing just fine. She on vacation until next week, so you guys are stuck with us. Can y'all take care of us till she gets home?" Adonyjah asked.

The three children looked at each other, puzzled. "Yeah," said Zayne, "but y'all gotta listen." They sat on chairs and bar stools; some shared seats with the children. The laughter from the children filled the air as they embraced freedom. Aryn sat Zayne on her lap; she hugged and kissed him. She couldn't remember a time when she felt like this.

"Excuse me, I wanna say somethin'," Adyson interrupted the mass of voices. Adonyjah took his spoon and tinged his glass to get order. Alyxander rolled up his napkin, pretending it was a microphone. Adyson took the rolled napkin with his head hung in embarrassment and placed it on the table. "I, uhm, I—"

"Use your mic," they yelled.

Why did I do this? Adyson thought, fumbling to refold the napkin. "I, uh, uhmm... wish all of you a prosperous year, with all your heart's desires met. I wish a peaceful life for these kids. I also hope I won't disappoint you guys. Oh, and thanks for having me with you."

"Happy New Year's," Aryn said, taking the napkin, "Ya know I've never been close to any of you jarheads, but it feels so good being here. I wish for us to be closer as a family, that I'll be a betta mother, auntie, daughter to Bree, and nicer to you guys."

"Amen, amen, I hope so too," Alyxander shouted.

"Be quiet, Alyx." She threw a piece of bread at him. "I also hope I'll meet a decent man to love me and my son." The tears rolled down her face. She placed the napkin down and dropped her head down Zayne's back.

"I'm gonna give you a big hug, Mommy," Zayne said, turning around, hugging her. Aryngton walked over and wrapped his arms around his twin. "I'm sorry, Aryngton," she whispered when he stood up. He rubbed her shoulders and picked up the napkin, "Happy New Year's. I hope that Adyson and Aryn receive their heart's desires. I hope ZaBryna'll come home rested and in excellent health, mentally and physically. I hope Avery will go on a long vacation, so we all can relax. I hope that we'll develop a better relationship with God. I love y'all."

Everyone raised their glasses, cheering; Adonyjah and Alyxander wrestled over the napkin, as the children laughed hysterically. They'd never had so much fun with their uncles and aunt.

"Donny, you're the eldest, you go last. Can't you see the pattern?" Alyxander explained.

"What pattern? The second child went first, then the youngest," Adonyjah responded. He tried not to laugh as he snatched the napkin and put it on the table to continue his explanation. "Then t—"

"I want for New Year's for my mommy to come home,"

screeched Symaya, as her uncles tried to grab the napkin from her. I want a Princess shirt, roller skates...and uh—"

"Girl, this isn't Christmas. Tell us something you want from your heart."

"I want Beena to smile," she said, with pride.

"Me too!" Zayne and Sayvian shouted. The room went silent; everyone was stunned. As much love as ZaBryna poured into them, they felt her unhappiness. Adonyjah stood up and handed Alyxander the folded napkin, hoping it would give him time to compose himself. Alyxander pushed it to Devon.

"I pray this year brings these babies their hearts' desires. I pray we'll grow spiritually and also, that we'll prosper, be healthy, stay close, find love, and be joyous. Thank you all for loving me, in spite of my lifestyle." He handed the napkin to Alyxander.

"God's at work in our family. I'm feelin it. Me, Donny, Devon, Zavian, and Aryngton have been prayin' for this; our prayers are being answered. This year I pray we'll grow spiritually; it's been an amazing adventure for me. I want us to do it as one in the body of Christ. I pray also that we'll find love, enjoy good health, prosperity and unity. Haze, welcome home, man; it's gonna be a great year."

Adonyjah took the ragged napkin. "This has been a great day; God is awesome! I wanna thank God for protecting us last night; it could've gotten real ugly in that camp. He protected Breena, 'cause that could've been worse too. And I wanna thank Him for each of you; it took growth for us to stand united. For this year I pray for unity in Christ, our health, prosperity, love and our hearts' desires to be blessed. Also, I pray we'll be reconnected with Adryannah and for us to grow spiritually."

"Man, get up." Alyxander elbowed Zavian.

"Y'all took the good ones. Seriously, I pray we get betta eating arrangements." They laughed. "I've known you all since preschool; so, I don't have to tell you, you're family. Thank you for reciprocating my love and trust. I piggyback on everyone's prayers and I wanna add that Breena'll find love and happiness and that Avery'll be healed and delivered." Everyone put their glasses down except Devon and the kids. I also pray for healing, so forgiveness can begin."

"Amen!" Devon shouted again; the children followed.

"Devon, *sit down*," Alyxander demanded, hitting the table. "I'm getting sick of this forgiveness crap."

"And you, Zavian, how you gonna ruin all our good wishes with that craziness?" Aryn snarled.

"Forgive him for what? He ain't sorry!" Aryngton shouted. Everyone looked at Aryngton, shocked that he stormed out.

"I got him." Devon stood up.

"Naw, I'll go," Adonyjah said. "Maybe I'll talk myself into forgiveness by helping him."

Zavian somberly sat down next to Aryn, taking her, and Adyson's hands. "We've got to forgive him, and that's hard." Adyson stood up, pulling his hand away. "Look, y'all just accepted me back, sssso, I'm not gonna rock the boat arguing."

"Adyson, ya can't just shut down 'cause you don't agree," Alyxander said. "We're tryna get a betta life. That can't happen if some of us are expressive and others aren't."

"Let's talk about this later," Zavian concluded, "and just enjoy ourselves, now."

⚬⚬⚬

"Listen, you three, Uncle Zave's goin' to set up the Wii for you," Aryngton informed them, "and we're going to have a meeting. We need y'all to play nicely and share, Symaya. I'm gonna put this timer on; when it rings, it's the next person's turn. Now Symaya, if you don't give the remote over when the bell rings, you'll no longer be allowed to play."

"You know your niece." Adonyjah chuckled.

"She's just like her mother, and you don't help her 'cause she's got your nose wiiiiiiiiide open."

"Screw you!" Adonyjah laughed, playfully punching him in his chest.

"I wanna thank you guys for getting me to see the importance of family, because we could've missed out on God's blessings," Adonyjah said.

Adyson raised his hand. "I'm thankful, but I'm having a real problem seeing this as a blessing. Our mother's in the hospital, and Avery's goin' to jail. I mean, we're a messed-up family, myself included."

"Adyson, look at those children's faces. ZaBryna could've been killed; but she wasn't. She was still in trouble and none of us knew it, but now we're able to do something about it," Adonyjah explained patiently. "You and Aryn are here, hanging with us. All of those things are blessings, because things could've been worse."

Adyson thought about the day before. His day had begun horribly. He was on his way to some shelter. Where? He was clueless. He shook his head and acknowledged what Adonyjah meant.

"I gotta get back to the house to clean up; I need some help. Stud, I hate to put the kids on you again, but it's best if we keep them out until it's clean.

"I can help, Aryngton," Aryn offered.

"Girl, who are you?" Alyxander asked, pushing her playfully. You got something you wanna tell us?"

"I'll help with the cleanup," Adyson said.

"Me too," the rest volunteered.

"Devon, you've been gone all night. Where's Trazie?" Zavian asked.

"Zay, mind your business. If Devon and Aryn wanted to tell us where their men were, we'd know by now. We ain't got no secrets." Adonyjah snickered, elbowing Alyxander and Aryngton.

Adyson shook his head in amusement. He liked what he saw between his siblings. *Man, I wanna be a part of this.*

"Donny, you're always instigating." Aryn paused, "Well, I guess, now is just as good as any time to talk to y'all about it. Jarvis and I broke up. I've been living in my car. But I'm fine. I've been going on job interviews, so hopefully I'll get a job soon, save and get an apartment."

Adonyjah sat down on the steps, and dropped his head in his hands.

"Well, I'm gonna take the kids to Chuck-E-Cheese, if it's open, and have lunch there." Aryngton said, "I know it seems like I'm always running when things get stressful, but I'm not. If we don't get a move on, we'll lose this day."

"Good. When we finish, we'll meet you there. How 'bout bowling?" Alyxander suggested.

"That sounds great, if it's open," Aryn agreed. "Donny, is that okay with you?"

"Did you all hear what Aryn said? I'm sitting here tryna figure out how a couple lives together, and the woman ends up on the street."

"Donny, please," Aryn assured him, "I'm fine. Let's just have fun."

"Aryn, does he know you're liv—"

"Donny," Aryngton interrupted, "let's deal with this later. We need to get started before it gets late."

Adonyjah stood and threw both hands up in the air. "Fine, if you don't want me to know, I'll mind my business."

Aryn wrapped her arms around her brother's waist. "Donny, I wanted to tell you, I just didn't want to ruin the holidays. Don't be angry, okay?"

Adonyjah put his arms around his sister's neck and laid his chin on top of her head. Alyxander snapped a picture, "I don't think I've ever seen any of us hug our sisters, so this is a cell-snap moment. Aryn, you're moving in with me, and Adyson, the devil has lost his reign over this family!"

❧ 12 ❧

NEW YEAR'S DAY

"Happy New Year's," Parris sang when Marian answered.

"You too. You sound funny."

"I'm a little... uh, you uh, know... uh, upset about you and uh Mama Rita."

"Don't sweat that. Ms. Thang'll get over herself," Marian responded.

"Marian, this isn't about her; it's about you and uh, your lack of respect for people. I invited you because I didn't want you to be alone on the holiday. I'd think after everything you've gone through, you'd run from married men."

"Pssh, why? Because they're stupid, allowing their hoochie-wives to punk them into returning home?"

"It's that kind of thinking that makes you do these things. Rita opened her home to you, and your gratitude was to try and do her husband? You'll never meet someone decent, if you keep chasing married men. You also make people not want to be bothered with you because they can't trust you."

"Gurl, please; I couldn't care less about women and their issues. If they kept their men satisfied, they wouldn't have to worry about me. And as far as being trusted, I'd have to give a crap about it to make a change."

"If I'd known you were going to act like that, I'd never have invited you."

"Well I didn't twist your arm, Parris, did I?" Marian responded, distracted. *Hmm, that's the SUV that Zavian got into yesterday.* Listen Parris, I gotta go; gotta put these kids down for their naps and run errands."

"You're not leaving them alone, are you?"

"Uh-uhn!"

"Marian, I'd like you to go to church, I—"

"Parris, I go to church every Sunday; me and God got it goin' on, believe that!"

"Mar—"

"Gotta go," Marian interrupted, hanging up. Marian looked out the window again. *That Parris got a lot of nerve, insinuating I need church. I hate when people act like I don't have a relationship with God.*

⚜

I SHOULD'VE NEVER INVITED HER; KINGSTON DIDN'T WANT TO, BUT I ignored him. Parris washed the dishes; her heart felt heavy, "Why do I grieve for her children? No one else in the family wants to deal with them."

"Hey babe," Kingston said, looking around to see who his wife was talking to. He hugged her from behind, kissing the nape of her neck. He could feel the tension rippling down her back. "Oww, what's got you so balled up?"

"I called Marian, and uhm..."

Kingston sighed. Parris walked out the kitchen, leaving Kingston to follow her.

"Go 'head, babe. I'm listenin'."

"Kingston, you always ask me what's going on, and then sigh when I'm tryna tell you. That's annoying."

Kingston dropped his head and looked at the designs in the carpet. "Babe, I'm frustrated with your relationship with Marian; you're always so troubled. Then you stay away from she for a while, and then go right back, tryna help she. She never apologizes, and y'all never discuss da problem. Ya me wife, I hate to see ya taken advantage of. Her own parents don't fool with she."

Parris hung her head, knowing her husband was right; but, Marian was alone with three children. "I'd just like to help her become a better person. Is that wrong?"

"No, it's not. The ting is, ya can't help someone who don't wanta change. Only Jesus can. Marian was allowed to do what she wanted as a child; she parents always made excuses for her. When parents do that, those behaviors become worse as de child grows up; then dey develop other tendencies to accommodate their negative behaviors; it's like a cancer. He took her hand. "I wish you'd leave she alone before she really causes ya grief. You should've known betta den to invite she to our family's house."

Parris leaned her head on Kingston's chest. She knew everything he said was true; but, she still felt she needed to encourage Marian. *There's hope for her; she's never messed with Kingston, so there has to be some good.* "Kingston, I believe Marion leaves those kids alone in the house. I was thinking, maybe we could take the kids sometime, and give her a break."

"Jesus, help us... Parris! Are you listening to yourself? Last night, did anyone know her past? No! Did she try to hit on Poppasan? That man's old enough to be her father!"

"Honey, we could do a trial with the girls, that way I could talk to Marian beforehand, make her understand that we'd help more, if she'd get herself together."

"No! I'm sorry, but I dun't want Marian in my house. I dun't want she children around ours. Now, if you wanna go to her house to take care of dem kids, there'll be no problem here."

"Kingston, this— Happy New Year's, Arjasyah," Parris answered, after checking the caller ID.

"Happy New Year's, sis. We're going to Ayden's house till Tuesday. You guys coming?"

"I think we can go."

"Go where?" Kingston interrupted; Parris ignored him.

"Princess, I'm sorry about Marian. I don't know why she acts like that."

"She's a wench!" shouted Kingston, patting Parris' behind.

"Kingston, that's not nice," she retorted, swatting his hand away.

"Princess, my love," he said, taking the phone from Parris, "my wife's perturbed because I dun't want that wench around my family. Anyhows, where we going?"

"Ayden's house."

"I'm feeling a yes, but me wife's rolling she eyes at me; so I may have to beg she."

"Kingston, it's New Year's; why are you aggravating her?" Arjasyah laughed.

"Un-uhn. I'm just tryin' to make she understand that she needs to leave Marian alone. How you gonna try to cluster a woman's husband right in front of she, in she own house; amongst she children? Parris always trying to save that girl, but she ain't tryin' to get saved; she's an evil wench."

"Randal told me about her, but that's Parris, family-oriented. It's hard for her to see her alone with kids. I'll talk to her."

"Thank you."

"No, thank you, for not falling prey to that woman's advances."

"That Randal has a big mouth, I see."

"Your secret's safe with me. So y'all coming?" Arjasyah asked again.

"Let me see what de wife says."

Kingston had always entertained Arjasyah. He moved to Maryland from the islands when he was three-and-a-half. His strong, cultural demeanor displayed itself when he was in trouble, or angry. However, he made it clear that while he wore the pants in his house, Parris was Chief-of-Operations in the Fine family.

"Tell my brodas, we'll be bowling later."

"Kingston, where's Parris?"

"She in the shower; she told me to tell you we can go. What time we leaving?"

"Uh, at four; you think you'll be ready?"

"I's born ready, but I don't know about yur sister and she kids."

"Goodbye, Kingston," Arjasyah sang.

"Goodbye, my love!"

੭੩

"I'M MARIAN. IS ZAVIAN HERE?"

"Sure, come in. I'm Aryn." She smiled, extending her hand, but her gesture was ignored.

"Hey Zavian," Marian said, hugging him as she scanned the

room. She could feel the excitement rise in her loins as she was introduced.

"What do you want, Marian?"

"Oh, uhm, I wanted to see... I mean, wish you a Happy New Year. I uh... uhm, didn't know you had company."

"This is my family. That's Aryn, Zayne, Symaya, and Sayvian. Over here are Devon, Adyson, Aryngton, Alyxander and Adonyjah."

While everyone was acknowledging her, Marian had zoomed in on Adyson and Aryngton. She walked over to Adyson and took his hand, turning his palms to face her. She traced the lines in his hands with her fingers, never taking her eyes off of his. *Hmm, I've never had a baby by a man with hazel eyes.* Adyson slowly pulled his hand from hers and left the room.

"So Aryngton, you have a girlfriend?" Marian asked, seductively.

"Uhm, uhm, no."

Marian walked slowly around Aryngton running her hand up his arm. "Wow, you sure are—"

"Marian," Zavian interrupted, "we're getting ready to leave. Can I do something for you?"

"Uh-uhn, I believe you blew your chance," she said, turning her attention back to Aryngton.

"Do you know that these guys are brothers?" Aryn snatched her wrist, when she reached for his chest. What are you doing, tryna play them? Are you crazy or just stupid?"

"Why, *you* want one?" Marian snapped.

Aryn stared at Marian, abruptly released her wrist and walked away. "I'm sick of you whores throwing yourselves at my brothers."

Adonyjah went to the kitchen and leaned on the door,

observing Adyson. He was amazed how much he had become concerned about him. "Hey bro, you okay?"

Adyson lifted his head from the table. "Man, Donny, I gotta get my life together; I don't even know if I'll succeed. The last thing I need is some woman throwing herself at me, reneging when I get excited, and I do time for doin' nothin'. I'm scared. I ain't cut from the same cloth as y'all. Do you realize last night was the first time I was angry at Avery? How do you reach my age and not see anything wrong with your mama suffering?" Tears rolled down his face. "How could I have been so stupid?"

Adonyjah sat next to Adyson and placed his arm on his shoulder. "Adyson, what do you mean you still served time for doin' nothing?"

"Huh? Nothing, man, nothing. I just don't need to send mixed messages."

"Haze, man, you gotta talk to me; you know I'm here for you. We're gonna help you get through this, no matter how long it takes. And you need to be patient with yourself," Adonyjah said, patting his brother on the back.

❧

Janet Florenton released the blinds, screaming as she ran to the door and flung it open. She grabbed Kenya; but, before she could be released, Kenya's father, TJ snatched her up in the air.

Her eyes met Tiffani's startled look, as Conrad Patterson snatched his pregnant daughter, lifting her. "Conrad, put her down; my God, she's pregnant!" Carol Patterson scolded.

Finally, both girls were placed on their feet, their faces held captive by their fathers. Kenya wiped the tears as she remembered how her father kissed every inch of her face. Tiffani's mother tugged her away from her father's embrace.

"'Cuse me. I'ms three, dis my daddy; him name's Trevor, like me. And my mommy's name Tiffani." Carol dropped her hands from Tiffani's arms, and methodically moved to the two waiting visitors. "Hi, little Trevor, I'm your grandma Carol; this is your grandpa Conrad."

"Trev-J, this is Mommy's mommy. Later today, we'll take you to meet my mommy."

"Can we take dese grandmas and grandpas to meet our odher ones? Pleeeaaaaase, Daddy?" Trev-J said, reaching his arms to Carol. She took Trev-J to the kitchen for snacks, while the others went into the living room. Tiffani and Trevor sat on the love seat, his arm protectively around his wife. Conrad elbowed TJ proudly, nodding his head in their direction. Kenya sat on the floor next to them.

"I gotta go to the bathroom," Tiffani said, motioning Kenya to assist Trevor with helping her up. Kenya leaped to her feet like they were going somewhere important.

"Baby girl, you're not going to have that baby here, are you? You're looking like you're gonna bust." Conrad laughed.

"No sir," Trevor answered. "We're due the end of February."

"Lawd, she's big!" TJ exclaimed. "Do they know how big that baby is? That can't be healthy."

Trevor hung his head. "They're twins." Conrad and TJ jumped up. "*Twins!*" They hi-fived each other, and then Trevor. "Dis calls for cigars. Come-na, we must get some," TJ said, getting their jackets, and summoning Trevor. "Yes mon, dis a man thang; we must do it together."

"I just need to let Tiffani know I'm leaving."

"The wives can tell her."

Trevor followed them to the door, and then stopped. "No disrespect, but I need to wait for Tiff so I can tell her myself."

"Oh, no problem," Conrad said, raising his eyebrows at TJ, who shrugged his shoulders.

"Gurrrl, I can't believe the greeting we got." Tiffani grabbed Kenya's wrist like they were back in high school, half jumping in a circle.

"I can't believe our parents are having New Year's dinner together. What's that all about?"

Kenya asked.

"They hated each other when we were kids," Tiffani answered. "And what about our dads, acting like we're some kind of princesses." They stood for a moment looking at each other, and simultaneously laughed.

"God is great," Kenya said, as tears washed her face. "Tiff, I was petrified coming here; I didn't know what to expect."

"SO WAS I. WELL, WE BETTA GO BACK SO THEY WON'T THINK we're talking about them," Tiffani suggested.

"Wait," Kenya said, grabbing her hand. "Pee first so me and Trev don't have to haul you up again."

"Haul? Really, Kenz, you couldn't think of a better word?" Tiffani scolded.

"Uh-nnn-no, in three months we'll pull you. Don't be ashamed of the truth," Kenya teased.

Trev-J was on the floor playing with the men when they returned. The women were in the kitchen. Kenya and Tiffani both stood leaning against the door smiling.

"Hey, babe." Trevor looked up smiling, "They want me to go with them to get cigars."

"Cigars?" Tiffani repeated. "Y'all don't smoke, do you?" She looked at her father and then at TJ.

"Uhm, it's to celebrate us having twins."

"They've nothing else to waste money on?" Carol said, wrapping her arms around both girls. "My baby's having babies." She smiled, touching Tiffani's stomach with tears rolling down her face. Tiffani wiped her mother's tears with her thumb. Kenya joined her mother in the kitchen.

"Mom, thank you for welcoming me and my family home," Tiffani said, hugging her.

"Baby, I'm glad you came home. We were worried sick about you; wondering what kind of man you married. He seems wonderful. I'm proud of you, honey; despite your daddy's and my drinking, you did well. It's been two years, and finally we're sober. I wish we could've done this when y'all were kids."

"Mom," Tiffani said, hugging her, "we're all where we're supposed to be, as God intended. I want you and Dad to be part of my children's lives." She placed her mother's hand on her stomach.

"Conrad, leave that child alone," Carol scolded.

"What? I was just telling TJ that he"— he pointed at Trevor —"is waiting to get permission from Tiffy. So I wanna know who wears the pants in the house?" Conrad and TJ laughed, grabbing Trevor's shoulders, rocking him.

"Babe, don't pay them no mind."

"I'm fine, honey; they don't know it's called, consideration."

"Consideration." Conrad and TJ laughed hysterically, "You's a sissy-boy," TJ ribbed.

"C'mon, let's go," Trevor said, extending his hands to help both men up.

"You guys should learn from Trevor. Baby, you're doin' right by my little girl; that's all that matters to me," Carol said.

"Thanks, Mrs. Patterson."

"Okay, Mama's boy," TJ teased. "Next you'll have stilettos on."

"You don't study them. They're jealous 'cause you know how to woo your woman," Janet added, placing the turkey on the table. Kenya followed behind, shooting Tiffani a confused look.

"Hmm, I gotta go to the bathroom. Kenya, can you help me?"

"Who are these people?" Tiffani asked as soon as she shut the door. Kenya sat on the tub and looked at her best friend leaning on the vanity; both wiped their eyes. "So many milestones we deprived them of because we hung on to the past, and feared returning. Trevor was right the first two years he wanted us to return." Tiffani cried, "I just thank God this time we listened to him. Mom and I apologized to each other, but I haven't spoken to my dad. It's nice seeing our parents accept Trevor."

"Yeah, he's soaking it up; it's like they've always known him. And our dads... cigars?" Kenya raised an eyebrow. "Mom and I haven't talked; I don't know what to say. Somethin's strained between us."

"Gia, we had to get away because if we hadn't, only God knows where we would be now. Unfortunately, we probably scared our parents to death. Apologizing will open the doors," Tiffani assured her. Kenya wiped her eyes and patted her leg, acknowledging acceptance of her advice.

৩৪৩

"MOM, I'M SORRY FOR LEAVING HOME THE WAY I DID; I KNOW you must've been worried sick." Kenya hugged her mother; Janet did not respond.

"Well Kenya, your dad was worried, but you know my philosophy: outta sight, outta mind."

Kenya grabbed her chest and gasped for air. "What are you saying?"

"I'm saying once you were gone, I moved on. You don't cry over spilled milk, Kenya. You wipe it up, rinse the rag and move on," Janet retorted, walking out the kitchen.

Kenya slowly lowered herself into the chair, absorbing the blow from her mother. She wasn't used to her surprise attacks anymore. She had always believed when she returned, she'd develop a better relationship with her parents. Now reality was staring her in the face. She'd never attain a mother-daughter relationship. She raced to the bathroom when the doorbell rang and leaned against it, hand over her mouth, stifling her cry. "Open up, Gia." Tiffani whispered.

Kenya opened the door and pulled Tiffani in. "I was praying everyone would've grown the heck up," Tiffani ranted, "What happened?"

"Uhm...she said she believes in 'outta sight, outta mind.' Said she moved on."

"After four years that's the best she could do? Let's go!" Tiffani snapped.

"Tiffani, wait. We can't. Think about Trev-J and your parents; they're so happy."

"You're beet red and you say you're okay? Uh-uhn, we gottta go."

"Tiff, Trev-J? He's enjoying his grandparents. I think we sh—"

"Kenya, open up; it's Dad," TJ announced, concerned.

"Now, what am I gonna do?"

"Talk to him," Tiffani responded, opening the door.

"What's happened baby?" TJ asked, pulling Kenya into his arms.

"Uhm... nothing. I think I'm coming down with something."

"Kenya," Tiffani scolded. "She apologized to your wife; her response was she believes in out of sight, out of mind. She said she moved on after Kenya left."

TJ rocked his daughter in his arms. "Aw baby, your momma struggles with forgiveness, always has."

"Dad, I don't need reasoning; I need her to stop hurting me. I need her to love me."

"Deep inside she does, sweetie," TJ said, sincerely.

Kenya lifted her head off her father's chest and looked at him. She felt sorry for him, he never saw Janet's flaws.

"I'm leaving. It was a mistake to come here. I only came 'cause I thought we could mend our differences, but I see now that's useless. You justify mother's behavior. I can't. It hurts too much for me to understand; it's sicker for me to attempt to."

"And what about me, honey? Do I have to endure that loss again?"

Kenya dropped her head trying to search for another alternative. "I'm sorry, I no longer have to deal with her. You can't handle her, so as always, there's no protection."

"Let me talk to your mother. *Please*, Kenya," TJ begged.

Kenya looked at her father, then at Tiffani who was waiting for her decision. She hated to ruin everything, but she didn't want to stay.

"Gia, don't worry about Trev and me. Whatever you decide, we'll do."

TJ put his arm around his daughter's shoulder. "Stay. I promise you, everything'll be alright."

❧

"THANK YOU FOR INVITING US," TAMMY, TREVOR'S MOTHER said, sitting next to Tiffani. "How many months are you?"

"Seven-and-a-half." Tiffani pulled Tammy's hand to her stomach to enjoy the activity inside her. "Feel your grandchildren misbehaving?"

"Grandchildren?" exclaimed Tammy.

"Yep," Trevor proudly confirmed, sticking his chest out. Conrad and TJ hi-fived each other and included Trevor's father and brothers. Trevor followed along, enjoying the fact that this made him the *man*. Until he met his father-in-law and TJ, twins weren't a big deal.

"Y'all are corrupting my husband." Tiffani laughed.

Kenya sat in the corner of the room smiling. New Year's couldn't have been better for the Bowen family. In spite of her mother, she felt family was the best security.

"Kenya," Javari, Tiffani's brother shouted, interrupting her thoughts, "when you contributing your addition to the family?"

"Kenya?" Janet snarled, "she knows nothin' about nurturing no baby, much less raising one." TJ shot his wife a warning look. "My baby's gonna be a fantastic mother once she meets Prince Charming."

"Sure will. Kenya was our nanny from the time Trev-J was born until this year. So when Prince Charming is approved by me, my children gonna have some cousins," Trevor concluded.

"Tiffani, will you need help with the babies?" Tammy asked. "I can come down for a week or two."

"Me too," Carol offered.

"Trevor has two weeks off and then Kenya'll be taking her

vacation. You all are more than welcome to stay as long as you want. I think I'll need all the help I can get."

"What hotels are near you?" Carol asked.

"Ma, you'll stay with us." Tiffani laughed.

"There's enough room for everyone between both houses," Kenya reassured.

"Should you be taking off under the—"

"Mom," Patrice interrupted, "don't start."

"Patrice, I don't think asking a simple question suggests starting something. What do you think, Tyrone?" Janet asked.

"Janet, let's try to have a good time," Tyrone responded, calmly.

The tension continued to thicken the air, regardless of what was said. Kenya's presence disturbed her mother. Kenya wanted to leave, but she wanted to see her brother, Kymanni. However, when she implied she would see him on her next visit, Janet lost her self-control. "Well you'd think since you haven't been here in so long, people wouldn't matter to you, or you to them." She sat upright in the chair and stared at Kenya, forcing her to feel uncomfortable.

She glanced at her father, who was engaged in conversation with the men and then slowly passed her eyes across the room at the women, cooing over Trev-J and Diandra, Kenya's niece.

"Mother, what's the problem? Should I leave? You seem upset. I'm not here to cause problems."

"Actually, Kenya, I'm bothered by you coming here uninvi—"

"Janet, may I speak to you?" TJ interrupted and grabbed his wife's wrist.

"Tyrone, I'm speak—"

"I think you've said enough," he snarled.

Kenya sat back trying to join in the women's conversation, but she was too jittery. Her mother had won. Tiffani sat next to her, holding her hands and squeezing them. Looking at her friend, she could see their visit was a mistake.

Patrice knelt at Kenya's feet. "Kenya, please don't let Mom keep you from coming back. You and Kymanni's absence has taken a toll on Dad."

"Gurl, please. As long as Dad has you and your mother, he's happy," Kenya lashed out.

"I know you think you know what goes on, but you don't," Patrice whispered.

"I don't have to know, I lived it," Kenya snapped.

"Gia, I'm not tryin' to argue..."

"Then shut up," Kenya snapped, storming out the room. Tiffani and Patrice raced behind her before she could close the bathroom door. Patrice had made up her mind she wasn't losing her sister again. When she was young, she enjoyed being the center of attention, but it cost her, her siblings. She lost communication with both when they left home. Diandra's father, Tristan found them. Kymanni reconciled with her; Kenya wouldn't.

"Get out, Patrice!" Kenya snapped.

"Kenya, I'm sorry for everything, including Mom's behavior. For years, we've talked about how things would be if you returned."

"Who's we? It can't be you, 'cause you always enjoyed me getting trashed by Mom, and Dad not protecting me. I knew it was a bad idea to come here, but in my heart I wanted to be—"

"Kenya," Tiffani intervened, "I know your mother's acting crazy, but I believe Patrice is sincere."

"Then *you* talk to her," Kenya shouted, storming out the door.

🦋 13 🦋

HOLDING ON

The train ride to Manhattan seemed long. Kenya looked out the window and thought about calling Tiffani so she wouldn't worry, but she was still too angry. "I'll call later," she mumbled, ignoring her vibrating phone. She had one stop to her destination with intent on boarding the next train to Maryland. *There's no more talking, forgiving, or tryin' to understand my parents.* "You chose them for my parents, so obviously, You feel I deserve them. Since You know all things, then You know I'm done with them."

Kenya walked to the McDonald's at Penn Station, purchased seventy-five dollars' worth of five-dollar gift certificates and then she purchased her ticket. The train was departing at eight o'clock. She sat on the bench, contemplating what she would do for the next half hour when her phone vibrated. "Yeah Trev, huh?" She sighed. "I've got my ticket; I'm leaving at eight."

"Kenya, we went looking for you. Where'd you go?"

"I caught a cab to the train station. I shouldn't have come. You all enjoy yourselves. I'm fine. I'll see you when you get back. Oh, can you bring my suitcase?"

"Kenya, please. I've been talking to TJ; he wants to sit with you and your mother to clear the air. I can come get you."

"Sit with us? I don't have a problem with her; she has a problem with me. I can't change that, nor am I tryin' to anymore. I'm done." The tears streamed down her face. "Trev, gotta go; love you guys," she said as she hung up. Kenya walked outside the terminal, pulled the gift cards from her purse and gave a few out as she felt led. *It's not much, but at least a few can get a meal for the holiday.*

She shook her head at the dilemma of the homeless and thought about how blessed she was. She had a job, a home, food, heat, water, and money. "I'm blessed with family: Tiffani and Trev," she whispered to herself. Her eyes burned, fighting tears that wanted to take authority. *Most of all, I have my health and p—*

Peace of mind had not cleared her thoughts completely when she felt a pang in her chest, turning her thoughts to her mother. The air was snatched from her. She stumbled and grabbed the lamp post. "I do have peace of mind," she cried. "If it wasn't for that witch You chose to be my mother, I'd be complete."

"You okay, miss?" the disheveled man asked, gently holding her arm.

"I'm fine, thanks." She smiled. "Here. Happy New Year." She extended her hand, giving him two gift cards. *In his own dilemma, he found compassion for me.*

"Thank you. God bless you, and remember, He's in control and makes no mistakes."

"God bless you too," Kenya replied, feeling guilty about even mentioning God's name, when seconds ago, she was pissed with Him. Kenya observed the man walking down the street, smiling and waving to people. No one returned his smile. Some looked at him with disgust; some whispered to their companions; some simply ignored him.

Kenya gave the last four gift cards to a pregnant woman with two small children. She walked back to the terminal, trying not to think about the woman's situation. Again, a feeling of gratefulness surged through her. *That could've been me.*

⊗⊛⊗

"KENYA'S STILL SELF-ABSORBED!" JANET SPURNED.

"You were out of line, Janet. For God's sake, she's our child, woman. I cannot understand why you still won't give that child a break. I can't take it anymore and I blame myself for not acknowledging this problem when they were kids. We've lost two of our children," TJ argued.

"TJ, stop making this a problem. Patrice turned out okay and we've got a beautiful granddaughter."

TJ stormed up the stairs. Reaching the top, he decided nothing would change until he did. He packed his belongings and moved into the guest room.

"Hey Mama, we're gonna stay here tonight, since the baby's asleep," Patrice said, walking into the living room. "Where's Dad?"

"Upstairs. You can stay in the guest room; your father bought a crib. The sheets are in the bottom drawer."

"Oh great. I don't want her getting in the habit of sleeping with me. Is Dad okay? It's kinda early for him to go to bed."

"He's not asleep; he's pouting."

"About Kenya?"

"Stay out of grown folk's business, Patrice," Janet snarled.

"Mother, you've gotta stop this thing with Kenya, for God's

sake. What did she do? Aww," Patrice cried out, clapping her hand over her mouth. "Is she adopted? She told us that when we were kids, but I didn't believe her."

"Who in the world did she tell that to?" Janet sneered.

"*Mother*, is Kenya adopted?" Silence engulfed the room. Patrice no longer felt the weight of her sleeping daughter.

"Kenya isn't adopted," the deep voice penetrated the airwaves from the top of the steps. Your mother feels Kenya's birth interrupted our lifestyle. She was born eight months after our wedding," TJ said, slowly descending the stairs, glaring at his wife. "Isn't that so, darling?"

"Don't start, Tyrone," Janet snapped.

"Is this true, Mother?" Patrice inquired in a begging, tell-me-this-isn't-true tone. An invasion from her tear ducts forced her to walk up the stairs, shaking her head without waiting for an answer.

"Are you satisfied?" Janet snarled. She looked her husband up and down twice, before noticing his suitcases. "Where do you think you're going?"

"Sit down, Janet, we need to talk," TJ snapped, surprised at his tone.

Janet sat with her mouth open, stunned by her husband. In their twenty-seven years, he had never raised his voice at her. Her first instinct was to chastise him, but TJ's glare stayed fixed on her; his finger remained pointed at the sofa. Instead she dropped her head, stared at her hands, fiddling.

"Patrice," he yelled, "Come here, please." He then addressed his wife. "I'm leaving for Maryland tomorrow to see if I can repair the damage that's been done to Kenya. I'm not losing her again. I take full responsibility for the dysfunction of this family and the loss of our children. I've always allowed you to spew your venom, but no more. So I expect while I'm gone, you will re-evaluate your effect on this family to see what you intend to do."

"TJ, what nonsense are you talking about? Kenya needs to grow up. She shouldn't have come here without calling first—"

"So, mother, should I call before I visit, too?" Patrice interrupted as she descended the stairs.

"You're putting words in my mouth, Patrice."

"What exactly are you saying, Janet, because I don't understand. You're always accusing Kenya of being selfish and controlling; yet it's you, you're describing."

"TJ, how can you say that?"

TJ sat on the sofa next to his wife and put his arm around her. "Look, I love you, and I'd kill myself before I did or said anything to hurt you. But I can't go on like this. This family has been destroyed because I failed to take my place as head. Honey, this isn't how it's supposed to be: three grown children, and only one will have anything to do with us. Kenya and Kymanni have done well for themselves; yet, we don't have a relationship with them."

"TJ, I don't know what you're talking about. Our children were treated equally and if they choose to have nothing to do with us, that's their problem. I couldn't care less."

TJ slowly stood up, releasing his wife's hand. "I care and I can't continue to pretend I'm comfortable with this." He picked up his suitcases and walked towards the door.

"Daddy, when are you coming back?" Patrice asked.

"I don't know, I need to spend time with your sister and straighten out this mess."

⚜

"GOOD AFTERNOON, LADIES AND GENTLEMEN. THANK YOU FOR

traveling the Northeast Regional 1-8-3 to Washington, DC. Please check your belongings. We'll be arriving in Trenton, New Jersey in 4-3-2-1 Now," the friendly voice sang. *"Have a wonderful New Year!"*

Kenya opened her eyes and looked around. She rubbed her eyes, checked her watch and then looked out the window. *Hmmph, my new year already started terribly, so I know what kinda year this is gonna be.*

"Excuse me, uh, miss, do you mind if I sit there?"

"Uh, no," Kenya replied. Shifting her legs into the aisle, she allowed the man's entrance to the seat by the window.

"How ya doing today?"

"I'm okay."

"Pretty lady like you should be better than okay." His smile extended itself across his face.

Kenya looked at the man. She had no idea what she was going to say, but he was going to know he should leave her alone. His smile was as warm as the sun. His dark eyes looked like they could be black. His dark brown, wavy hair was cut low; his smooth covered-in-mocha complexion glowed evenly. His nose was wide to fit his oval shaped face. He was gorgeous.

"I'm great, how are you doing?" Kenya smugly replied.

"Oh, I'm blessed and highly favored."

Kenya released a forced grin. "Well that's wonderful." To avoiding further conversation, she turned her head to face the aisle and closed her eyes. *I wonder what it feels like to be blessed. I'm not sure if I'm blessed, but I'm definitely not highly favored. Would I feel it? Is a person extremely happy because of this favor? How did God choose who deserved favor?*

"Gooooood evening ladies and gentlemen. You're traveling Northeast Regional 1-8-3 to Washington, DC. the nexxxxt stop... Wilmington, Del—"

Kenya's eyes opened and she abruptly sat up. She stretched her arms forward and then covered her mouth with both hands to smother a surprised yawn.

"Well hello, sleepyhead. You have a good nap? Maybe you better tell me where you're going so I can make sure you don't miss your stop."

"I'm fine, thanks."

"I hope you don't think I'm trying to stalk you." Her friendly neighbor chuckled.

"Nope, that's not it."

"You... I—"

"Look sir, I don't want to be rude, but I'm really not in a good mood, and I don't feel like talking to anyone. So please, if you—"

She stopped and answered her phone. "Hey, Zavian. Oh thanks, Happy New Year to you, too! I'm on Amtrak as we speak."

"Who's picking you up?" Kenya's lack of interest in him stemmed from him changing women like he changed clothes. *I was so stupid; I didn't even think that if I wanted a good woman I needed to chan—.*

"It'll be late. I'm catching a cab," Kenya said.

"No, I'll pick you up. What time are you arriving?" he asked.

"Did Tiffani or Trevor call you?" Kenya asked harshly. She sighed when he didn't answer. "I'm arriving at twelve-after-eleven. I told you, it's gonna be late."

"I'll be there at eleven sharp," Zavian responded. "Traveling mercies; see you when you get here."

Kenya smiled. Even though she could never click with Zavian as a boyfriend, she loved him as a friend. He was a better friend than he could ever be a boyfriend because he was loyal and trust-worthy. "Ok, big head." She laughed. "I'll probably need your company after the day I had."

"You wanna talk about it?"

"No, I'm fine; I always am."

"I love you, Kenzee-babe. I'm here for you."

"Thanks Zee, love ya back. See you later." She hung up the phone, her smile now genuine, grateful. She didn't have to catch a cab. She thought about the women who foolishly became romantically involved with Zavian. *They're deprived of knowing the great guy he really is.*

"I'm glad to see speaking to your boyfriend made you feel better," her traveling neighbor said.

"He's not my boyfriend," Kenya snapped. "He's a friend."

"Isn't that what boyfriend means?"

Kenya looked at him and smiled. *Had I met him before I knew Jesus, this communication he insists on having would've ceased.* "Sir, I don't wanna be rude, but I've had a rough day. Do you mind if we make this a no-communication trip?"

"Oh, I don't mind; although, sometimes it's better to communicate about our troubles to help sort them out. We can get a better understanding," he replied, smiling.

Kenya found herself wanting to be patient with him. *Poor thing, he's crazy.* "That may be true, but I don't know you."

"Oh that's easy to fix. My name's Daniel John Davidson. He extended his hand and waited for Kenya to respond. "I live in New Carrollton, I'm single, no children and thirty-three years young." He laughed as if he had just told the funniest joke.

What the heck, I might as well enjoy myself, because I don't need to be sleeping. "My name's Kenya Florenton. I live in Clinton, I'm single, no children and not telling my age." She placed her hand in his and laughed at the simplicity of their conversation.

"Well there is a beautiful smile hidden behind that scowl," Daniel teased.

"I don't have a scowl; I have things on my mind. Look, if I appeared rude..."

"If? Are you kidding me?" Daniel continued teasing. He enjoyed watching Kenya's disposition transform, because he could feel her pain in his chest. "I'm just messing with you, you weren't rude; but, I could tell I invaded your peace."

"So you got jokes; I'm so far from peace. If I had wanted to maintain peace, I would've stayed home."

"You know, there's always a justifiable reason why we do things, and why things happen." Daniel explained, "Nothing that happens in life is senseless or a mistake. A week, month, or years from now you may understand the reason for your visit to New York. You'll say, "I'm thankful I went to New York, even though my peace was stolen." Daniel smiled, satisfied that he'd made Kenya aware of this small, but important fact.

"I always tell my friends to make a note of the date an event happens, whether it's fulfilling, tragic, crazy, whatever; then when the revelation comes to them, I tell them to be mindful of how long it took. You can even do this to see how God prevails by watching how He responds when we trust Him."

"Yeah, well I'm gonna try that, 'cause there are things I've asked Him to fix in my life that He just hasn't seemed to have gotten around to. Don't get me wrong, I'm thankful 'cause He's kept me safe and provides. I guess that's all He finds worth doing for me."

"So you're mad at God?"

"Did I say I was mad at God? I believe the word I used was thankful. Um... Daniel, is it? I've had a rough day. I need to be by myself." She smiled.

"Hey, I understand and I'm not trying to bother you. Close your eyes and rest."

"Thanks." Kenya squirmed to find the right position and closed her eyes.

"You know," Daniel interrupted, "sometimes, it's we who have to change before God can help us. I mean, it's like we want change, but we don't want to do any changing ourselves. So we should surrender our—"

He stopped when Kenya's head snapped in his direction. "Look, I'm not trying to bother you, I'm just trying to say I understand where you're coming from."

"You understand where I'm coming from?" Kenya growled. "You don't have a clue what's going on."

"No, I don't," Daniel answered calmly, "but I can feel your pain. I'd like to help, that's all."

"And you can help," she paused, "by leaving me alone."

"Ok, I'm sorry," Daniel said, sadly.

"Thank you," Kenya snapped, turning her back to him. She stretched her arms, settled into a relaxed position and closed her eyes.

"Gooooood eveee-ning ladies and gentlemen. You're traveling Northeast Regional 1-8-3. *We'll be arriving in NEW CARROLLTON, in 4-3-2-1 Now!* Have a wonderful, blessed and safe holiday."

"Wow. You didn't get to rest," Daniel said, smiling.

Kenya stood up and stepped into the aisle. She picked up her bags and walked towards the door in silence.

"Look, please forgive me. I wanna give you my business card. If you ever just need to talk."

Kenya took the card and headed towards the escalator.

14

FORGIVENESS IS A FUNNY THING

"Father, I'm sorry for straying and not making You head of my household. Please forgive me. I, uh... I need Your help with Kenya and restoring my family." TJ sighed, "I'm ashamed to even ask for favors." The fumbling at his door interrupted him, so he opened it.

"Hi Trev-J, how are you?"

"What chu doin', Pops?"

"Uhm... actually, I was praying."

"You yike God? He's Mommy's, Daddy's, and my best friend, too. I yike pwrayin' to Him 'cause He yisens. Daddy said, He's my Big Daddy and Zesus is my brodder; I yike Him too." He climbed up in TJ's lap and continued, "One time when I was yittle, I hurted my fingers weal bad." Trev-J touched his finger as if the pain were still there. "My mommy said, 'Ask God to stop the pain,' and so I did, and then He *did*. And, one time—"

"Tre-vor De-la-no Bowen, why are you in Pop's room?" Tiffani scolded, knocking on the door.

"I not bodder him, he opened the door for me 'cause he was yonely and pwrayin'. He yikes God too, so I was asplainin' 'bout God."

"Boy, go to your father."

"I'm sorry, Mr. Florenton; he's so excited to have other people in his life besides his dad, Kenya and me."

"Not a problem, and call me TJ or Pops. Have you spoken to Kenya yet?"

"Naw, I woke up praying about everything. I feel bad that our visit went the way it did, because we were so excited."

Tiffani sighed, "We should've left with her. I think that's what we should've done. I thought she was going to the hotel Trevor reserved." She lifted her head and met TJ's teary eyes. *Lawd, pleaaase don't let this situation destroy our friendship. I know Kenya; she'll say I betrayed—*"

TJ touched her hands. "It's gonna be okay. Maybe I need to stay at a hotel."

"Absolutely not," Trevor said, knocking on the doorframe with Trev-J sitting on his shoulders. You'll stay here as long as you need to."

"I don't want to cause any problems. Kenya and Tiffani have been friends too long."

"Then nothing should be able to destroy that friendship. They're both still the same people they were when I met them; they'll get through this," Trevor said, taking his wife's hand and giving it a reassuring squeeze. "Well I think I better go visit and have a talk with my sister. Babe, you wanna join me?"

"I'll stay here and prepare breakfast."

"Chicken," Trevor teased, kissing her on the cheek. "I already made breakfast. Everything's in the microwave. Leave the dishes."

"You're not having breakfast with us?" TJ asked.

"It depends how much crow your daughter's gonna make me eat." Trevor laughed. "God, help me."

❧

"So, do you think Kenya will come?" TJ asked.

"I don't know, she's pretty stubborn; however, so is Trevor. But he has a way of making a person see something positive in every situation. We just have to wait and see what she's gonna do."

"Auntie Gia," Trevor squealed, running to meet her at the door.

"Hey, man." Kenya picked him up and buried her face in his neck, hoping to smother the turbulence that consumed her. *Trevor's right. I need my dad to heal, just as much as he needs me to forgive him. That doesn't mean Trevor always has to be the voice of reason. How dare he ask me if I sought God in my decision not to speak to my dad. I'm not tryin' to help him clear his conscience.*

Speaking to him would free both of us and I want... no, I need his guilt to eat him alive. She put Trev-J on the floor, closed her eyes and prayed, then stood up straight and grabbed Trevor's extended hand, following him into the kitchen.

"Good morning, everyone," Kenya mumbled, hugging Tiffani.

"Hi, Dad." Kenya bowed her head, avoiding eye contact. "What are you doing here?"

"Hi, baby girl. I wanted to see you... uh, maybe talk a little," TJ responded, nervously. "Are you okay?"

"I'm great. Well, I got a lot to do, so I better get goin'," Kenya announced, trying to ease the tension in the room.

"Gia, I thought we could go somewhere and talk before you begin your day," TJ pleaded.

"Uhm... we can go to my house." Kenya stared at Trevor,

contemplating a plan that could get her away from all of them. Her mind was blank. She walked out the kitchen to the family room, hugged Trev-J and walked out the door. She gave no indication her father should follow.

❃

KENYA OPENED THE DOOR WHEN TJ ARRIVED.

Forgiveness...the gift that opens the gateway to the blood of the Lamb, for God's mercy, grace, and healing. God, help Kenya to forgive so she can begin to heal from everything. Help her to turn to You so she can find comfort in Your love and be freed from the bondage of unhappiness. Lord, I pray we did the right thing bringing Pops down here, guided by Your will and not ours. In Jesus..., Trevor prayed within, after walking TJ to Kenya's house.

TJ looked around the room, admiring his daughter's living room. He enjoyed the abstract painting hanging over the mantel and the family pictures of Tiffani, Trevor, Trev-J and Kenya. Yet as his eyes roamed the room, he found no pictures of their family. Her walls defined his failure as a father. Wiping the tears from his eyes, he wondered how he'd ever reconcile his family.

"Lord, I need you. Pleaaaaase guide me in this matter. Reconcile and redeem my family. Forgive me, in Jesus' name, Amen."

"Baby girl, I wan—"

"Don't call me that," Kenya sneered.

"I'm... uh... sorry, Kenya. I've always called you that, don't you remember?" TJ scrambled to meet her at a point comfortable for both of them.

"Yeah, I do; but I was never your baby girl; Patrice was. Oh yeah, your princess too, that's what you called her."

"Kenya, honey, I... uh. I...," TJ stuttered, searching for words to bring calmness to Kenya's agitated state.

"What purpose could there be for you intruding on me? The reason I left by train was so I wouldn't impose on anyone; now you impose on my family." She hit her chest to emphasize Tiffani was her family. "I should've never come to your house uninvited. I apologize for that."

"Gia, you don't ever need an invitation to my home."

Kenya laughed. "Are you serious? You can't be serious. That was never my home, it's not even your home. Ya just haven't accepted that it's Janet Florenton's, maybe even Patrice's home, but it's never been mine, Kymanni's, or yours. Ya just pay the bills associated with it."

Her venom caused TJ's skin to crawl; his face winced. TJ stepped back and leaned against the wall, searching for something to say. *This is what we've made our daughter, Janet: bitter and loveless. Whatever I have to do, Lord, whatever I must endure, give me strength, please. Just give me the strength.* "Kenya, I'm sorry."

"Sorry? What are you sorry for?" Kenya shouted, ignoring the conviction in her spirit. She was going to make her father pay for all of her disappointments.

"I'm sorry for not protecting you and your brother. I'm sorry that I can't take the pain away," TJ cried, grasping Kenya's hand. "I wish I could undo and fix everything, but I—"

"Stop. It's too late for that. When it was important to me for us to reconcile, y'all were too happy I disappeared outta your lives. I have no mother and no father. So you wasted a trip, 'cause I'm not walking back into that bull—"

"Kenya," TJ scolded, "that's enough. Whatever I've failed to be as your father, I won't allow you to disrespect me. I came here because I wanted to apologize. I can't change the past. All I can do, with the help of God, is work on the future. I wanna help you heal. Baby, I don't know what else to do. Tell me, Gia, what I should do and I'll do it." He reached for Kenya's hand again, but she pulled away.

"You don't have to worry about me cursing ever again, because I've nothing else to say to you. I don't need you to help me heal. I accepted the mistake of my birth a long time ago, so I don't need you." The tears streamed down both of their faces. "You and your wife have been dead to me for years. I don't know why I allowed myself to be pulled into nonsense, but I'm over it. I'm not gonna allow myself to be a victim to you people, *ever again*. Now I've got work to do. You can let yourself out," she finalized, walking to the guest room and shutting the door.

TJ pulled his handkerchief from his back pocket and wiped his face. He walked slowly down the hall and left. Crossing the street, he stopped to look up at the living room window, hoping he'd catch a glimpse of hope. Kenya was not there.

⚜

KENYA LAY ACROSS HER BED AND CRIED HERSELF TO SLEEP. When she woke, the street lights were shining through the window, reflecting themselves on the door. She walked to the kitchen and poured a glass of juice and sat in the dark. *How could Tiffani bring that man down here? How could she allow him to stay at her house? I can't forgive my parents. Shoot, it actually felt good watching him grovel; he reminded me of my childhood, beggin—*

"Kenya, open the door," Trevor shouted, ringing the bell. She slowly walked to the window and looked at her walkway. She could see the back of Trevor's head. She stood motionless, staring outside. She never noticed that Trevor used his key to enter. "Kenya?" Trevor said softly, standing in the doorway. "You okay?"

"Yes," Kenya whispered, tears trailing down her face. He pulled out a chair and sat beside her.

"Do you wanna talk?" She shook her head no. "Your dad's pretty upset; he didn't think his visit would upset—"

"How could you all betray me like this? Y'all are supposed to be my family," Kenya cried. "I trusted you."

"Gi." Trevor wrapped his arms around her. "You know we'd never do anything to hurt you. We were thrilled that your dad wanted to do right by you; we thought you'd be too. This is a good thing, if y'all talk. He realizes he was wrong; he wants to make amends. We thought that's what you wanted."

"In case you missed it, I wanted their love when I went to New York and did I get it? *No!* Didn't you see the way I was treated?"

"Kenya, I don't know what happened, exactly, but I know your mother was the problem, not your father."

"Not my father? My father's the clone of my mother. If she says or feels it, his opinion's no different."

"When you left, your father and I went looking for you. Your father confronted your mother."

"Ha, you expect me to believe that?"

"No, I expect you to believe *me*. The man came here with three suitcases. Gia, please, you'll feel so much better, if you'd just talk to him. He knows he was wrong."

"I'm not gonna forgive him, if that's what you're tryna get me to do, Trevor. I'm not!"

"Sis, I'd love for you to forgive them, but I know right now, that's too difficult. Plus, you forgiving your dad is between you and God. I just want you to talk. It'll help ease some of your pain."

Kenya stared out the window so long, Trevor thought she'd fallen asleep. Then without anything being said, she turned her tear-stained face towards him and hugged him. "Nothing he can say will change the way I feel."

"Kenya, this isn't about your mother," Trevor assured.

"Trev, it's always about my mother, that's what you don't understand. TJ Florenton does nothing without her approval. *Nothing.*"

"Talking to him will help you."

"You think I should feel better because of his efforts?" Tears streamed down her face as she sighed. "The first half hour, I'm treated like a princess, then my mother sideswipes me with verbal attacks. The greeting was fake, a setup against me. And now you think I should feel better because he came down here, pretending he wants reconciliation?"

"How could they have plotted against you when they didn't know you were coming?" Trevor stood up, pulling her into his arms. "Kenya, your dad had nothing to do with your mother's antics."

She tried to pull her head off his chest, but he gently held her head in place. "Your mother has some deep-rooted issues. The last thing Tiff and I want is for her personal handicaps to infect you. You don't have to forgive him right now, just hear what he has to say. Forgiveness will come later."

"No, *no*, Trev. I'm done with this. Look, I've got to get up early tomorrow and these people aren't worth me losing sleep over." She pushed herself from his grip and walked him to the front door. "Tell Tiff I love her and kiss Trev-J for me."

"Kenya, let me just say this... forgiveness is one of the most difficult things to do because of the violation of your heart. At the same time, it's the only way a person can completely heal. Think about it. Who does our healing come from? Huh, Gi?" Trevor was speaking fast, hoping something he said would touch Kenya before she shut him out. "I think they all work together, because forgiveness is mandated by God and healing, joy and happiness are His gifts to us."

"I know you don't wanna hear this now, but you've got to pray and ask God to help you forgive your parents. This will demolish Janet's power over your happiness. You need forgiveness to be free from the violator's beck and call. Unforgiveness deprives you of life."

❦

"SHE'S MAD, TREV," TIFFANI CRIED.

"She not mad, she's upset." Trevor tried to make light of Kenya's three days of silence. She hadn't called, nor did she return their calls.

"I'm serious, Trevor, I'm due in five weeks, and my sister's not talking to me."

"How do you know she's not talking to you?" Trevor asked, pulling her into his arms. "She may just be busy."

Tiffani pulled from his grasp, "Have you ever known Gia to be so busy that she doesn't come for dinner or call, especially with me nearing the end of my pregnancy. She's angry. Stop downplaying this situation, Trevor!"

"I'm trying to keep you calm, baby. You know you can't be getting upset like this."

"Not allowing me to talk about this problem is upsetting me. I don't need a doctor, Mr. Bowen, I need my husband."

"Look, just give Kenya time, she'll come around. She's not angry with us, she's angry with her parents, especially her dad, for coming here. I'll go over and talk to her this evening when she comes home." Trevor pulled his wife back into his arms and kissed her.

"You do know she's been coming home late every evening, don't you?"

"I know. I'll call and see when she's available. That's all we can do until Kenya decides she wants to talk. We'll just have to be patient until she's ready."

❧ 15 ❧

YOU SHOULD BE HAPPY

"**M**arketing, Kenya speaking. May I help you?"

"Wow, I couldn't believe you actually called. Left a real number too." Daniel laughed.

"Hello, Daniel," Kenya replied, unamused with his comments about calling. "How are you?"

"I'm great, now that you've called."

Why did I call this idiot? He's crazy. "I shouldn't have...uhm called—"

"Look Kenya, I'm sorry. I was trying to lighten up the mood, but I can see you're uncomfortable. What's going on?" Kenya could hear the concern in his voice, but her guard was up. She wasn't going to revert, trusting her decision to call him.

"Kenya? You okay?"

"Uhm... I'm sorry, this was a bad idea."

"Kenya, wait! Look, I'm sorry for upsetting you. It's uh, just that I'm happy you called." Daniel inhaled deeply, "Uh, it's in your voice, you need to talk. Do you wanna go out to lunch?"

"I don't know... can I call you back?"

"You know you won't call back. Let's do dinner, that may be easier. What da ya say?"

Kenya held the phone tightly, shaking her head from side to side, trying to think of an excuse to get out of the dinner. "It's not a date, just dinner. We can drive our own cars, okay?" Daniel assured her.

"There's a Shrimp and Rib Shack in Clinton. Is there one near you?"

"Don't worry about me," Daniel replied.

Kenya hung up the phone and leaned back in her chair, considering what she'd wear. She wasn't interested in Daniel, he was just a distraction to keep her out of Tiffani and Trevor's reach.

Daniel opened the door, kissed her on the cheek, and gave her his seat as they waited for a table. He leaned against the wall, watching Kenya twirl her hands around each other. He wondered what could've happened to make such pain pour out of one person, and plunge into another. The pain was stronger than the day he met her. *I can see my work's cut out for me. Thank you, Lord, for making me a vessel."*

Kenya stared into the tank housing the lobsters, thinking she felt just as trapped in her own life. She had forgotten about Daniel until he called her name; she gave him a half-hearted smile, before following him to their table.

"I'm glad you called, Kenya. I haven't stopped thinking about you since we met."

"Listen Daniel, I'm not interested in dating. My life's a mess and I don't wanna complicate it more."

"I'm not hitting on you. You seem like you need someone to talk to; that's why I insisted on dinner. However, if you don't wanna talk now, that's fine. But I do have great listening skills."

"Well, I appreciate that, but right now I'm tired of people's opinions. I just wanna embrace peace, if that's possible." They ordered their food, which came quickly. Kenya ordered a salad, too nervous to eat anything else. Daniel decided on the Tilapia dinner. "So Daniel, what do you do?" Kenya asked coyly, trying to keep the conversation away from her.

"I'm a personal trainer with a small gym in my basement. I don't have a lot of clients, but I'm able to maintain, doing something I enjoy."

"That's wonderful. I think a person should always do what they enjoy, especially since they spend most of their waking hours at work. Do you have a lot of female clients?"

"I do, mostly women in their forties, struggling with weight. That's why maintaining my gym in my home is important. My fees remain reasonable. It's like giving to my community. What about you, what do you do at the bank?"

"Uhm, I'm in Marketing. Yep, that's what I do." She felt nervous.

"You don't sound like you enjoy what you're doing," Daniel responded, choosing his words carefully.

"Mmm, well it's a job. I'm grateful to have one in these trying times. Thankfully it pays well enough for me to meet all my needs."

"Do you enjoy what you do?"

"Uh." Kenya chuckled, nervously, "For me that's not important. I'm just trying to sustain, not be self-gratified." She looked down at her hands, scolding herself for prying into his livelihood.

"Are you saying you shouldn't be happy with your job?"

"Uh, no, I'm not saying that." She looked at her watch. "Wow, it's late. I've got an early meeting tomorrow."

"Yeah, me too... well, I don't have a meeting, but I do have an early-morning session." They wound up staying a bit longer and spent the remaining time talking about the things they enjoyed doing and about their relationship with God.

⚜

KENYA WALKED THE TWO LONG BLOCKS TO HER HOUSE. SHE HAD parked there to avoid Tiffani or Trevor seeing her. It had been two weeks since Trevor's talk, and she planned to avoid any more with either of them. Closing the door to the foyer, she kicked off her shoes, leaned against the wall and closed her eyes. It had been a long day for her, especially since she wasn't one to hang out after work. She checked her watch, allowing the moon's light to shine on it. It was ten-thirty.

She walked down the dark hall that led to the family room, turned on the light and was surprised to find Tiffani slouched on the couch asleep. "Tiff." Kenya gently tapped her, not wanting to scare her. "What are you doing here?"

Tiffani yawned, extending her arms and stretching, indicating she'd been there for a while. "I, ya... uh." She sat up. "Where have you been, Kenya?" she inquired. "Do you know what time it is?"

"I do. The question is, why are you here instead of in your bed?"

Tiffani sat up, stretching from side to side, and then looked down at her hands. She reached over and took Kenya's. "I'm sorry. It was wrong for me to bring your dad back. I wou...I...would"— the tears streamed down her face, as she gasped for air to finish —"I'd never do anything to hurt you or jeopardize our trust. Please forgive me, forgive us."

Kenya slowly let go of Tiffani's hand and walked to the fireplace. "I'm not angry at you, or Trevor; I'm just upset. I don't understand how Trevor and especially *you* could think it was okay to bring that man here to surprise me. You h-h-hurt me. You know the problems I have with those people; they hate me."

"Kenya, we weren't trying to surprise you, and your dad doesn't hate you. He wants to make amends with you, and we wanted to help. He packed three suitcases, so it doesn't look like he plans on going home anytime soon. Evidently something happened between him and your mother, because Patrice kept calling constantly, trying to get him to come home."

"Tiffani, I couldn't care less about my parents' dilemma; they deserve each other. How can you say that you weren't surprising me when you didn't call me before you brought him? I'd never do that to you. *Never*," Kenya cried.

"Kenya, we called you repeatedly," Tiffani retorted, "but you wouldn't answer."

"So, you felt I—"

"I don't get it, Kenya," Tiffani interrupted. "You're always talking about what you'd do to have a relationship with them; yet, here you had the opportunity to get some answers from Pops, and you won't talk to him. We brought him home with us, because we thought it would help you." She poked her finger in Kenya's chest. "And now you're blowing it out of proportion. Please don't do this. I don't know what you want from me."

Kenya glared at Tiffani. "I want everyone to stay out of my business!" She covered her mouth trying to stop herself from dicing through her friend. From the look in Tiffani's eyes she knew it was too late; she'd hurt her.

Tiffani raised herself off the couch, and wobbled over to Kenya. She wrapped her swollen fingers around Kenya's forearm, and spun her around, "Kenya Florenton, I know your mother hurt you. This last time was probably the worse, because you were away for so long, and nothing changed—"

"Look Tiff," Kenya raised her hand, interrupting.

"No," Tiffani raised her voice, "you've ranted enough; now it's my time to speak. That crap your mother pulled was hurtful. Shoot, it hurt me because I love you. But what's more hurtful is you won't let me help you through this. Kenya, you must own the hurt, so you can forgive that woman. She's wicked, and your family has simply tolerated it. Everyone sucks it up and moves on until her next attack."

Kenya shook her head in disagreement. She kept her eyes fixed on the floor to control the tears trying to escape before speaking. "I can't... I'll be okay. I don't need anyone." She slipped her arm away from Tiffani's, and shifted her eyes towards the window. "It's late, Tiffani. I've got an early meeting."

Kenya followed Tiffani as she walked to the couch, helping her put on her coat. Tiffani stopped mid-way and looked at Kenya. "Are we okay?"

"We're fine," Kenya replied half-heartedly, her fake smile displayed. Her eyes looked past Tiffani.

"You're still going to be in the delivery room with me, aren't you? Kenya, I need you... it's in two weeks."

"I'll be there, Tiff," Kenya replied, abruptly.

"Why don't you come over for dinner tomorrow? Lil Trev misses you a lot."

"Hmm, I can't. Marian asked me to go somewhere with her," Kenya replied, shifting her eyes to the carpet.

"Okay Kenya, I'm done. I never thought anything could come between us, but I was wrong." The tears streamed down Tiffani's face. When she reached the front door, she turned and hugged Kenya. "I hope you'll be there when the babies come. I hope the love you have for me and my family supersedes the hate you have for your parents. I love you, Kenya." Tiffani sobbed, walking out the door.

Kenya watched her walk down the four steps, cross the street and enter her house, before closing the door. She leaned her forehead on the door, allowing the tears to flow freely down her cheeks. *Lord, what's wrong with me? Why am I hurting the people I love? I'm angry, and I don't know why.*

She slid down to the floor, cupping her face in her hands. *I know Tiff would never hurt me; she's always had my back. So why am I angry? Lord, help me, please. I don't know what's wrong—"* She pulled her phone out of her jacket pocket, and opened the line without looking at the caller ID. "Hello?"

"Did I wake you? It's Daniel."

"No, I...uh was just sitting... uhm, thinking. Did you want something?"

"Uhmm, I just wanted to thank you for having dinner with me—"

"No problem," Kenya interrupted. "Daniel, I enjoyed dinner too, but I'm not interested in dating.

"Kenya, I'm not looking for a relationship. I think you're a nice person, and I'd just like us to be friends—without benefits. I could tell since we first met you were going through something. Your spirit's in turmoil; I hear it when you speak." He took a deep breath. "Life's too short to carry the burdens of the world. You need to... uh, turn it over to God."

"Daniel," Kenya interrupted again, "it's late. Was there something you wanted?" The tears cruised down her face and she could feel herself getting ready to sniffle. *Can't let this man think I'm weak.*

"You're right, it's getting late; but before we hang up, I wanna tell you something. If you ever find that this burden you're dealing with becomes more than you can bear, promise me you'll call me."

The first sniffle slipped out before she could release a muffled, "Yes." The tears flowed down her face freely; her legs had stiffened in their drawn-up position. Kenya remained on the floor, and began to pray. "Help me," she cried hysterically, "pleeeease...."

⊗⊗⊗

KENYA VAGUELY HEARD THE ALARM CLOCK BLARING FROM HER room. She was surprised to find herself still sitting on the floor by the front door. She was in the same position she was when she hung up from Daniel. More surprising was the peace she felt. She sat quietly, enjoying the absence of turmoil. She felt a smile pierce through the corners of her mouth when she walked up the stairs to her bedroom.

Pulling her phone from her pocket, she sat on her bed and checked her call log. "Daniel." She sighed, pressed the Call button on his name and waited to connect.

"Hey, Daniel," she sang.

"Kenya?"

"All day." She laughed. She was shocked to hear herself sounding so vibrant; she was flabbergasted that she *felt* vibrant.

"Uhm, what time's your class this morning?" Kenya asked, sheepishly.

"Is everything alright?"

"Couldn't be betta." The laughter in her voice penetrated his earpiece. "So, what time's your class?"

"Oh, my client canceled last night, why?"

"Well, would you join me for breakfast at The Barrel?"

"The Barrel?" Daniel shouted, a little louder than he meant to. "Don't you have a meeting?"

"I called out. I haven't taken a day off in three years, so today won't be a big deal. So what diya say?"

"Breakfast it is." Daniel laughed, avoiding asking any more questions.

"Alrighty-then, I'll pick you up in an hour before it starts getting crowded."

Alrighty then? Who are you?

"Uh, Kenya, you do know The Barrel's in Waldorf, right? I live in New Carrollton."

"Well, give me your address."

After they hung up, Daniel sat up on his bed and stared out the window. He glanced at the clock on his bedside table. It was five-fifty. "Well Lord, please guide me throughout my dealings with Kenya, so that I won't be the cause of any setbacks. Speak through me so this day and her deliverance will be to Your glory. In Jesus' name I pray. Amen."

⚜

KENYA WATCHED WITH AMUSEMENT AS DANIEL CUT HIS pancakes into tiny squares. He had stacked them evenly, one on top of another, plastered butter on each without looking up once. She could tell this was a ritual for him. Daniel put down the syrup and looked at her. "So, Ms. Kenya, thank you for inviting me to breakfast. I'm honored."

"Yeah right," Kenya responded, but looking into Daniel's eyes, she knew that he was telling her the truth and for now she would trust him.

"I wanna apologize for the way I've treated you since we met."

Daniel extended his hand across the table to touch hers. She didn't pull away. "No apologies needed. You seem relaxed this morning, and for that I'm grateful."

"I do... I mean, I am," Kenya stuttered.

"So did you get everything straight with whatever the problem was?" Daniel asked, cautiously.

Kenya dropped her head, put some pancakes in her mouth, and lifted her eyes to meet his.

"Aw, I'm sorry Kenya, you—"

"No," she raised her hand, interrupting him, and took a deep breath. "Daniel, when you saw me on the train, I'd just come from visiting my parents in New York. I hadn't seen them in four years."

Daniel's mouth dropped and she raised her hand again, she had to get it out before she clammed up. "It was my friend's idea; he's like a brother to me. I went against my better judgment. Uhm...I, uh," Kenya dropped her head, and sighed. She shook her head trying to keep herself from crying.

"Kenya, you don't have to tell me." Kenya lifted her hand, "I'm goin' ta bust if I don't talk to someone. I just don't know where to start." She talked for two hours about her relationship, growing up with her parents and her sister. She told him about Tiffani, Trevor, Little Trevor and the twins that would soon be blessing their lives.

Daniel struggled emotionally with her pain as she described her relationship with her mother. When she finished, she looked at the customers and realized she didn't recognize anyone from when they sat down. "Wow, I guess I burned your ears, huh? I'm so sorry. I didn't realize I was talking so much."

'Girl, you needed to vent. That's too much stuff for one person to endure. Do you feel better?" Daniel inquired, smiling.

"I feel light," she giggled.

"Kenya, life's the second most precious gift that God's given us, after Jesus. Every day should be filled with God's love and new experiences that bring joy. After all, God's sole purpose for our lives is for us to bring glory and honor to Him. And we can't do that if we're bombarded with a bunch of *stuff*; you know, like anger, hurt, frustration, fear and disappointment."

"I don't know how to stop the disappointment, or the hurt," Kenya said, annoyed. *This is why I hate talking to people. They're always telling you what you're not supposed to think, or feel, blasting you with what God wants from us, and not telling you how to do it.*

"Sit down," Daniel said firmly, holding her wrist when she stood up. I can see you're annoyed with what I just said, but I wasn't chastising you. I'm explaining something. Think about what you did last night that dragged you out of that slump. Hmm, what's got you so bubbly this morning?"

"I prayed for God to help me. I wanna be happy. I'm sick of being angry all the time."

"You should be happy; we all should. Yet somehow, we allow people and insignificant things to rob us of this God-given privilege, forgetting to believe that prayer is bigger than anyone or anything. Prayer helps us to endure until God brings us through. I'm glad you prayed. Now you'll begin to heal, experiencing His joy and you deserve that."

"Yeah, well I also need to learn how to forgive." Kenya smiled sheepishly.

"You already started the process when you confessed it and prayed for God's help with it." Daniel chuckled.

16

THE BOTTOM LINE

Kenya jumped when the tattered box moved. Cautiously she lifted the box and peeked in. "It's a man," she whispered. "What's he doing in my yard? Oh Lord, help him. Whatever his needs are, bless him with them." *It's eighteen degrees out here. Where's his jacket?* "Guide and protect me, Lord. Amen. Sir? Sir! Wake up. You'll freeze to death out here," Kenya said, gently shaking his arm. The odor from his clothes choked her.

"Ooooow." The man stretched. "I'm up! Good morning. I'm sorry, I didn't mean to be here when you came out. What time is it?"

"It's six-thirty, morning time. C'mon, let me help you up. You must be freezing," Kenya said, pulling his arm, "Would you like some hot chocolate, or coffee?"

"Uhm, yes, hot chocolate would be great, if it's not a bother."

"Look, my husband's upstairs asleep. He's a cop, and was up late doing surveillance, so we have to be quiet."

"Your husband won't get angry at you for letting a strange man in the house?"

"Only if you do something stupid, like rob us. Then I'll never hear the end of it, and you'll be dead. Sooo, I'm trusting you're just a little down on your luck and need help, right?" Kenya confirmed, pointing her finger at him. The man nodded his head, smiling.

"You hungry?"

"Yes, ma'am, I'm starved, but I don't have any money to offer you."

"First of all, don't call me ma'am. I'm sure we're the same age. My name's Kenya." Kenya put her key in the door, pushed it open and stepped aside to let him in. "Have a seat," Kenya said, nervously, pulling out a chair for him, "I'm just gonna let my husband know you're here. I'll be right back."

When she returned she had two towels, a washcloth, a black Old Navy sweatsuit, a pair of socks, lotion, toothpaste, a toothbrush and a soap bar. All were still in their wrappings, and stacked on top of each other. She handed them to him. "Would you like to freshen up before breakfast?" she asked, pointing in the direction of the bathroom. "There's shampoo and conditioner on the tub, if ya wanna wash your hair."

"Oh that's great, thanks," the man said, smiling. He was astonished that she so generously extended her hospitality. He followed her to the bathroom, and before he closed the door, he thanked her again.

"Please, don't make me regret this, okay?"

"I won't. I deeply appreciate what you've done for me."

⚜

KENYA FINISHED SETTING THE TABLE, PLACING THE PAN OF biscuits in the center of the table next to the platters of fruit, eggs, grits and turkey bacon. She poured two glasses of orange juice, and then made his hot chocolate, and her coffee. Her mind drifted to the situation at hand: She had a strange man in her house. "Jesus, hmmph, I don't know why I want to help this man, but Lord, in my craziness, please have my back. Protect me, Lord, and bless our food that it'll be nourishment to our bodies, a—

"In Jesus name we pray, Amen," the stranger concluded her prayer.

"Sorry," she said, smiling sheepishly. "It's just—" The man raised his hand, interrupting her. "You would be foolish not to. I pray about everything; it's the only way."

"Sometimes I wonder if that's why there's so much tragedy in this world. The lack of prayer is the reason so many people remain stuck in their situations. People don't pray. Angels are sitting around with nothing to do, no one and nothing to protect. People are just wandering around with no direction. So you don't need to apologize to me for praying while you have some stranger in your house."

Kenya cleared her throat and standing, she rested her hands on the back of her chair, staring at him. This *dude cleans up amazingly well; he's gorgeous! His eyes, hmm, what a beautiful shade of brown, almost like they're swirled with cream. Lord, they penetrate my heart when he speaks. Nice height, solid build, broad chest and wide shoulders. Umph, umph, umph. Soap and water sure did this brotha justice. Aww, and his hair... I bet when that head is done, he is absolutely beautiful! Some woman will snatch his fine butt up!*

"Mmm, the eggs and this white thingy-thing are delicious."

"That 'white thingy-thing' as you call it is grits. I can't believe you've never had them."

"Never did. You know, I can't remember the last time I had a sit down meal either." He smiled.

"Wow, I'm sorry to hear that." Kenya inhaled deeply. "Soooo, we're sitting here having breakfast and I don't know your name." Kenya laughed nervously, revisiting the fact that she let a strange man into her home.

"Oh, I'm sorry. My name's Messiah, Messiah Emmanuel Jehovanah." He smiled.

"Yeah right, and my name," she placed her hands on her chest, "is Mary Immaculate," Kenya shot back, annoyed that he lied.

"Kenya, I'm serious. That's my name," he said, looking around the room, and patting himself, "My proof's in that brown bag I had."

"I put it on the counter in the kitchen," Kenya informed him.

When he returned he opened the bag, pulled out his passport and handed it to her. Kenya sat back quietly and looked from Messiah to the closed book.

"Go ahead, open it. I trust you."

"You trust me?" Kenya snickered. "Cute, real cute." She opened the passport and there, under Messiah's picture was his name, MESSIAH EMMANUEL JEHOVANAH. She closed the passport and handed it to Messiah, staring at him. "Your parents named you Messiah Emmanuel?"

"Well yeah, I guess because of my last name. I don't think they thought they were being disrespectful; my parents were good people, godly people.

"Well, it's not for me to judge. Where are you from?"

"Everywhere."

"Okay then, Messiah, how long have you been in Maryland?" Kenya asked, patiently.

"I arrived last night," Messiah responded, confidently.

This fool must've escaped from Saint Elizabeth. Jesus, Kenya! How could you let him in your home? You should've taken the food outside to him. No, no! Then he wouldn't have been able to clean up and he'd be freezing. She shook her head to stop the conflict in it.

"Kenya, are you alright?" Messiah asked, concerned.

"Am I alright? I'm fine. Are you alright?"

"I'm great," Messiah responded jovially.

"So where are you from, and why Maryland?"

'Well I was in New York yesterday. To tell you the truth, I'm here to find churches that meet the criteria of a godly Church. You know?" Messiah said, nodding his head proudly.

"Why are you doing that?" Kenya asked.

"WELL BASICALLY, TO SEE IF THEY MEET THE NEEDS OF THE people and are truly teaching what the Word of God says. You see, the churches appear to be falling by the wayside far more frequently than the world. Most of them have gotten away from the true teachings, resulting in many Christians forgetting what Christianity stands for. They've lost character and integrity in their quest to be churchgoers."

"Being homeless and observing, it seems that compassion and love are embraced more by those who don't go to church. It's not supposed to be like that. Most Christians are walking around thinking they're better than people struggling, homeless, straddling in their walk with God. I could go on and on. There's a handful who truly have the love of God in them. Some are even predicting, or as they call it, prophesying where people's souls are going to end up. This is truly sad because if they knew God's word and what's expected of us, they wouldn't be so quick to condemn the souls of others.

"I'm confused... are you, Jesus? What makes you think you have the right to make that kind of judgment? Yeah, there are problems in the churches, but how are you authorized to say which one's right or wrong? That's judging and that's God's job."

"You're absolutely right; however, I'm not judging. It's just that people are always bragging that they go to church, but most are just going through the motions; their hearts are far from it.

"I don't know, Messiah. Are you a preacher? Can you make that kind of assessment? Maybe you should worry about getting a job, and finding a place to live. I mean what can you do? Look, I grew up in the church, where I was forced for years to spend every Sunday in those pews, not understanding one word spoken. What I did learn was that I'd never please God, because everything I did while my eyes were open seemed to provoke Him. It seemed to me that my sins were more powerful than His Blood, which later I found wasn't the case. By the time I was old enough to make a decision to stop going to church, God wasn't even on my list as a friend.

"I spent years living my life in misery: doing dumb things with dumb people, involving myself in fake relationships, which included most of my family. Yet years later the church still prevails. Did they change some of their teachings? Probably not. I just know that a lot of people still believe in their teachings.

"My personal turmoil caused me so much pain, it forced me back to church. Looking back I know now that was God. It helped some, and then ultimately it almost destroyed me because of preachers' stealing and craziness. The first church I attended, The Church of the Righteous, was huge. One of the things that attracted me to that church was the dance ministry. The bishop held my attention when he preached; unfortunately, when his ministers preached, most of them seemed to be more interested in their own glory, rather than God's.

"Most of the members were in cliques. I don't know what common interests united them; all I know is I tried to get involved, but just didn't fit in. Eventually I left.

"Then I went to this church that was small. They met in a storefront. That was the first time I can actually say I *heard*"—she put both hands up to show quotes signs with her fingers—"the Word of God and it penetrated me. It made me wanna get my life together and have a personal relationship with God. It was awesome the way that preacher taught about God. I started reading the Bible on my own, because that was his biggest emphasis. 'You have to study to show thyself approved.' I can't tell you how many times he pounded that into our heads." Kenya sat hunched in her chair, reminiscing about how her life had spiritually changed.

"DAVENPORT WOULD SAY, 'YOU DON'T JUST SIT IN CHURCH ON Sundays and go back to business as usual the next day. You have to read that Bible; it's your strength, your rock. God's Word isn't confusing! So when you leave church, you should leave full, and in peace.' And we always did, every time we left service. He used to say, 'If you don't know what's in the Bible, how will you know if you're being misguided? If someone preaches a sermon that leaves you unsatisfied or confused, it's *your* responsibility to go to the Word of God, cross-reference and make sure the Word wasn't compromised.

"'Preachers aren't God, they make mistakes too. That's why you have to diligently keep us in prayer, put us before the throne.

The preacher is the first to be spiritually attacked. Always pray for me, as I pray for you.'"

"So when did he die?" Messiah asked.

"Who?"

"The preacher."

"He didn't die. Where did you get that from?" Kenya snapped.

"You," Messiah said, pointing at her. "You spoke about him like he died. What happened to him?"

"We didn't diligently pray for him. We laughed, not understanding he was dead serious or he was giving us a hint. Unfortunately, the church struggled with the minister and his wife's marital issues which eventually divided the church. He walked away from the church without any warning, leaving the few that stood with him and his vision, wandering aimlessly. He didn't even set us up in a church before disappearing. And to add insult to injury, he left us in debt because an elderly member allowed him to use her credit for the church." Kenya took a deep breath and laughed, looking at Messiah.

"Did you forgive him?" Messiah asked.

"Huh?"

"Did you forgive him?"

"Fortunately for us, he truly did allow God to use him when he was here. His teaching was so powerful that I knew how to deal with that betrayal and continued on with my relationship with the Lord. I also learned enough that I'll never be blindsided by another preacher," Kenya answered, matter-of-factly.

"Did you forgive him?" Messiah asked again.

"I just told you I did," Kenya snapped.

"When? You just started babbling that you were taught not to get blindsided. You never said you forgave him."

"Of course I forgave him. I fasted and prayed. I asked God to search my heart and reveal any unforgiveness that was hidden."

"Good for you, girl." Messiah raised his hand for a hi-five. Kenya slapped his hand weakly.

"I know forgiveness is important. Davenport taught us that. He also taught us the weapon to arm ourselves with, the Bible, and those lessons are far more valuable to me than what he did to our church." She leaned forward and gave Messiah a genuine smile. "I'm free, Messiah, in more ways than you'll ever know."

"Is Davenport free?" Messiah asked.

"You're a mess, you know that? Uh, when he was preaching at our church, he was probably in just as much bondage as we were. When he left he definitely was in bondage, at least we believe he was, because he wouldn't have lied and snuck out the way he did. He would've been a man and told us it bothered him that there were only a handful of us and he found something better than us, you know... financially more lucrative for him. We would've been upset, but it's a known fact that for most of these ministers, it's about the money, not souls."

"Hmm, is he free now?" Messiah asked again.

"Boy, I don't know; I hope he is. It would be a doggone shame if we all got free and he was still trapped in his crap, wouldn't it?"

"Did he apologize to everyone?" Messiah asked, concerned.

"Oh Lawd, please help me with this man. No, Messiah. He's too arrogant and self-righteous for that."

"So do you think he's still in bondage, and that's why he hasn't apologized to you all?"

"Messiah, all I know is that Davenport was in our life for a reason and God used him to free us. After we got free he went on to pick up some other man's church with lots of members. I'm still free. He taught us well. His season with us is over and ours with him. We've moved on, can you?"

"Oh my, that's a horrible thing to say! Don't you care about how that man is, spiritually?"

"Nnnno, there's nothing I can do about his soul, is there? I'm not Jesus, Messiah. All I can do is pray for him. Look, I'm tired of looking for a church that's about Christ, and I'm sick of preachers who are only about themselves, their family, and their financial gains. For most preachers, it's about the numbers. Their egos can't be stroked unless they have thousands of people, kissing their a—"

"Kenya, stop!" Messiah shouted, raising both his hands, astonished that this was how she assessed the church.

"Look, if you don't want me to sugar coat this, don't ask me anything. The last two churches I attended were worse than Davenport's. The first lady of one of the churches was overheard telling members that we were sitting in her church, eating up her *husband's* word for free. I left the church immediately 'cause they both knew we were left in debt and the members stuck together to pay off that debt. They said it was okay and paying off that debt was considered tithing. They blatantly lied!

"The one after that, Bishop Garrison, this dude was robbing his members. He spent hours begging for money from the men, women, children aaand the elderly. His wife's just as bad. Neither of them have jobs and act like all people have to do is sit in church every night to give them money. He's so crazy he assigns his flunkies to lock the church doors at service. They're financially raping their members."

"Wow." Messiah shook his head. "I can't believe you've gone through so much. Locking doors... that's not good, not good at all. Are you in a church now?"

"Yeah, for funerals or sometimes I go back to Garrison." Kenya laughed to break the tension. "Look, Messiah, all jokes aside I'm on sabbatical from church. They're too dysfunctional. I'm really tired of ministers, first ladies, and the Halleluiah crusaders, sanctified with themselves and unaware of how much damage they do to those truly seeking God."

"Forgiveness is too difficult to achieve to fool with folks who are intentionally destroying people, and then I still have to forgive them. I'm a mess by myself; I don't need anyone to help me sin. So back to you. You wanna check out churches to see if they are preaching the word of God. Am I right? How do you propose to help these churches? Do you really think you can change these preachers? Where would you start?"

"It's not that I want to judge or change the preacher, I want to help them make a difference. You can't change anyone. If I can help those ministers who strayed, I'll minister to them and direct them back to being laborers of Christ. I want to help the people who are sitting in the church being seat warmers, educate them about the importance of salvation. Do people love Christ? I believe they do. Are they changing? A lot of them are, but it's not enough to count it a success.

"Unfortunately, there are too many who don't even know they've got stuff going on with them. They have no conscience about the things that they do wrong and they're sitting right there in the church. There needs to be more conviction in the teachings for people to want to change.

"This is crazy, Messiah, this isn't even an assignment. Should I just escort you to the door now for safety?"

"Kenya, believe me, you've never been safer than you are right now."

❧ 17 ❧

WATCH WHAT YOU SAY

I *know Messiah's judging me for what I said about the church. Well I*
told the truth and he can judge me if he wants on the other side of
my door. Who is he to judge me anyway? He's homeless, not me.
People make me sick, always looking in someone else's back yard, never
looking in their own. Like their sh—

Kenya jumped at the touch of Messiah's hand on her shoulder.
"Stop worrying. You're giving yourself wrinkles." Messiah laughed,
rubbing the furrows on her forehead with his hand.

"We're just talking. I'm not judging you, okay?"

"What makes you think I'm worrying?"

"Awww, my spirit told me." Messiah laughed, clearing the table.

Kenya reached for her vibrating phone. "Hello?"

"Hey, gurl, how ya doin'?" Cassie Hunt asked.

"I'm okay, just a little tired. What's going on?"

"Wanna come to evening service with me and Marian?"

"Yeah, I'm gonna bring a friend."

"Who?" Cassie asked.

"You don't know him."

"Him? What him do you know that I don't know?"

"It's a long story. See you later."

"Wait. Is he married?" Cassie whispered.

"Uh, I don't know; I don't think so."

"If you don't know, why are you wasting your time with him?"

"I'm not talking to him. I'm just bringing him to church," Kenya snapped.

"Is he cute?"

"Goodbye, Cassie."

"Ok, what kind of car does he drive?" Cassie persisted.

"Later." Kenya hung up the phone.

"Good grief. That girl gets on my nerves," Kenya mumbled.

"Do you pray for her?" Messiah asked, putting the platter in the sink.

"She doesn't pray for herself. I'm still trying to figure out why she goes to church, other than to find a man."

"That's okay. God knows why. Pray for her anyway so things can change."

"The only reason I associate with her is because my bes... I'll just pray for her. So Mr. Jehovanah, would you like to go to the mall with me?"

"Do you have a Bible I can borrow later? I lost mine in my travels."

❦

"GET OUTTA HERE, YOU NEVER HAD CHINESE FOOD? WELL you're safe with the soup, vegetables, and this chicken." Kenya laughed. They returned from their shopping spree with most of the bags being Messiah's. At first he had battled with Kenya about her buying him the tennis shoes, coat and other items. "Do you have clothes other than those rags you had on earlier, and this sweat suit?" she asked. He shook his head no.

"Are you planning to look for a job?" she asked.

"Yes," he responded, hanging his head. "Pay me when you're rich," she concluded with a smile.

She didn't splurge on expensive things, but she wasn't cheap. She bought him everything he needed as far as winter clothing was concerned, not to mention men's shampoo, lotion, soap and shaving products. She even bought him a new leather-bound Bible. Messiah was amazed at her generosity to a stranger. He took off his coat and hung it on the closet's doorknob and walked into the kitchen. Kenya had already placed the food on platters, and was setting the table. "I was going to help you, Kenya," Messiah said, "I just need to use your bathroom again, if you don't mind."

"Yeah, I mind." Kenya laughed. "Boy, go on."

They kept their conversation light, talking mainly about the things they liked to do. Kenya talked about her job, and Messiah talked about what kind of job he wanted. They had become comfortable with each other. She no longer felt intimidated by him asking her questions.

"Hey, do you wanna go to service tonight? That girl that called earlier invited us."

"What did you tell her?" Messiah asked.

"I told her I might, and that I had a friend I'd like to bring," Kenya said.

Messiah placed his fork on his plate, and smiled. *The person who said she didn't trust anyone, considers me a friend.*

"What? Why are you looking at me like that?" Kenya asked, nervously.

"You consider me your friend; I can't tell you how blessed I feel. Thank you, I feel the same way."

"Stop playing, Messiah. I didn't mean boyfriend."

"I know that. You have a husband." Messiah smiled.

"Uh, yeah uh, right. So, you wanna go?"

"Let's go," Messiah replied, excitedly.

⚙

CASSIE CHECKED THE TIME AND CALLED MARIAN. "COME ON out, I'm at Kenya's. Please hurry up so she don't start complaining about tardiness."

Kenya and Messiah came out the door and walked up to the truck. "That's how he's going dressed?" Cassie asked.

"Messiah, this is Cassie, Cassie, Messiah," Kenya said, ignoring her comment.

"Good evening, how are you Cassie?" Messiah asked, smiling.

"Messiah? Who in the world named you that? Why would anyone name their child, Messiah?"

"Cassie! You really need to learn how to talk to people," Kenya scolded, climbing in the front seat.

"Hey, I wanna get some water and milk before we go to church. Can we stop at the store?" Marian asked, getting in the car with Jacinta. When she saw Messiah, she moved the baby over to her right side, extending her hand to shake Messiah's. "Oh hi! I'm Marian, and this is Jacinta."

"Marian," Kenya said, turning to face the back. "Where's Jacinta's car seat?"

"Gurl, I don't got one; it's not like I gotta car. So how'd you two meet?"

"Marian, you need a car seat for this child. It's the law," Kenya said, firmly.

"Don't start, Kenya, with your righteous, mumbo-jumbo, law-abiding-citizen routine, okay?" Marian scolded.

"Fine, it's not my vehicle; I won't be the one getting fined," Kenya snapped.

"Sooo, Messiah; how'd y'all, meet?" Marian asked, again.

"I was outside, when Kenya came out her house and we started talking," Messiah said.

"So is that the reason you didn't get a chance to change your clothes?" Cassie asked.

"What's wrong with the way he looks? I think he's fine," Kenya said.

"Well, I can't believe he's going to church like that on his first visit," Cassie continued.

"This is all I have," Messiah said, hoping Cassie would change the subject.

"I don't know, Mr. Messiah. That's sad, if that's all you've got. What in the world do you do for a living?" Cassie asked.

"Cassie! He's fine. The Bible says 'Come as you are,' now leave him alone," Kenya snapped.

"Yeah, it does say that; but it didn't say look a mess."

"Dag, Cassie! Are you trying to discourage him from going to church?" Kenya asked.

"No, I'm just saying, he sho—" Cassie began choking, and gasping for air. Messiah leaned over the front seat and touched her head; the choking stopped.

"That's what you get, gurl, for talking about this fine, chocolate-looking brothah. He looks fine to me." Marian laughed.

"Now, maybe you'll stop discouraging him," Kenya scolded.

"Don't worry, Kenya; I have thick skin," Messiah said.

"That's not the point. She could've discouraged someone else and there's enough discouragement in the church. A lot of people find it hard to walk through church doors the first time. Some are hung up on their size, clothes, anything; and people who profess to be Christians should be intelligent enough to know to shut their mouths."

"Okay Kenya. Messiah, I'm sorry for insulting you. Any friend of Kenya's is a friend of mine."

"Apology accepted."

"Marian, how long are you going to be in the store? You know the doors lock at a certain time. So don't be long, and take your baby with you!" Cassie said.

"I'm only getting bread and water, so stop tripping," Marian snapped.

"Oh, if that's all you want, I can get it," Messiah said, getting out of the car.

Messiah could see the girls from the window and contemplated ways he could get Kenya to trust him, so he could help her. He could see her as a team-player in whatever decisions he made for the ministry.

"Mmm-hmm, looks like you've got you a good one. Actually wants to get off his butt and do something. Now, if he'd just buy himself some clothes, I'd even work him," Cassie said.

"Cassie, you don't know what people are going through, especially today with the way the economy is. You shouldn't be criticizing," Kenya said.

"Eww Kenya, I didn't realize you liked him. That's why you all protective of him. Gurl, I ain't mad; I'd do the same if I found me a gorgeous man like that," Cassie teased.

"We're just friends."

"You can't see he's ffffffffffiiine? What's wrong with you?" Cassie said, winking at Marian.

"I'm not violating God again for any man, regardless of what he looks like. If the Lord doesn't hand-deliver someone to me personally, I'm not traveling down that road."

"Well do you mind if I take a shot at him?" Cassie asked.

"Go ahead. That man looks like he's got more on his mind than chasing skirts."

⚜

THEY ENTERED THE CHURCH AND LOOKED FOR FOUR SEATS together. Bishop Garrison Hughes was standing on the side of the front door, reprimanding one of the ushers. "He always makes a scene if someone upsets him so everyone coming in can see. Then he'll include it in his sermon," Cassie whispered to Messiah.

"Good morning, Cassie, Marian, and uh... uh, Kenya, isn't it?" Garrison greeted.

"Good morning, Bishop. This is my friend, Messiah," Kenya said, smiling proudly at Messiah.

"Well I hope you two aren't fornicating and will move your relationship in the direction of marriage. Then y'all can come see me, and I'll tell you if I approve of the marriage."

"Excuse me?" Kenya and Messiah bellowed in unison.

"Bishop!" Kenya exclaimed, "What right do—"

He raised his hand, dismissing her and slid to Cassie, taking her hand. "And how are you, Sistah Cassie?" He smiled, rubbing his hand over hers.

"Oh, I'm just fine, and you're looking debonair in that suit." The bishop let go of her hand, spread his arms out, and turned slowly. Cassie threw her head back and laughed seductively.

Marian laughed at them, looking to see if Mrs. Hughes was watching. *This dude's such a trip. Last week it was me he was screwing, till he came to my house and found out I had kids. Shoot, it's only three of 'em.* Immediately her thoughts turned to her first and only date with him. *Everything would've been fine had I been able to find a babysitter. I shouldn't have left them alone, especially since I didn't know his plans for that evening.*

After dinner we toured the National Harbor. Then we went to the Graylord Hotel. Our room was gorgeous. The king-size bed dressed in a dark blue comforter really accentuated the room with its classic composition of ivory, blue, and white gold, with walnut furnishings.

I was looking for a husband, not a screwing partner. I've had enough of those and all I've done is have babies with no ring in sight. I thought Garrison was a good prospect, but he was disrespecting me, saying he just wanted to have sex; and if he wanted to make love, he'd be with his wife.

So after trying to wake him several times, I took his car keys and money out of his pocket for my troubles and went home.

Two hours later that fool, Garrison banged on my door and laid on the bell like he was crazy. He stormed into my living room, calling me all kinds of 'B's, demanding his keys and money. I gave him the keys, but threatened to tell his wife about our little adventure if he pressed me for the money.

❦

EVERYONE STOOD TO WITNESS THE USHERS ENTERING. Following them were the ministers' wives. Behind them, six men surrounded the bishop, escorting him to the podium. The women were seated in the front rows, the ushers directed the ministers and bishop up to the platform.

Before he began speaking the bishop stopped and took a drink of water. Most of the faces of those in the congregation were awestruck, waiting in anticipation for his next move. "You'd think Jesus himself had stepped up to that podium," Marian whispered to Cassie, unable to contain herself. "I don't know how much more I can take of this, but I'm scared to leave because there's nowhere to go except home, stuck with them kids doing nothing."

"You trippin', this is fun watching how stupid people actually are; that's why I come," Cassie responded.

"Praise the Lord, Saints! God's doing mighty things in this place and I'm proud to be a part of it. I'm excited for the word, I's got today, but first I want to take care of church business." The bishop jumped up and down, acting like he had the Holy Ghost. People started clapping.

"It's time to give and let's make sure we give unselfishly, 'cause you're giving to God, not me. I don't need your money. I'm rich." He stomped his feet, rocking from side to side. "The basket to the left's the building fund; following to the right are the tithes, general offering, and the love offering."

"Remember now, God loves a cheerful giver. You give and you'll receive. If you don't have it, but have your rent and utility money stashed in your wallets, or deposited in your bank account, take out your checkbook. Give. You'll receive it back before that bill is due.

"If you're afraid to give, God will curse you for not trusting Him. Even if you have to sacrifice your grocery money, the money for your children's shoes, give. Whatever it is you have, give and remember it's not for me; it's for God. I got mine!" He patted his chest, his rings, extended their sparkle to greet the congregants.

Messiah cringed, and then turned his head to the back of the church, watching the line being formed. The tempo of the music filled the church as people eagerly walked up to the table, putting money in each basket.

When everyone returned to their seats, Mrs. Garrison instructed the congregation to give at least twenty-five dollars to the Media ministry. Once again the procession began, and when it stopped, she dropped the price to ten dollars. When everyone was seated, she dropped the price to anything less than ten dollars. She told the members to have each of their children give also. She instructed the children if their parents didn't have it, to ask other members.

"Are they kidding?" Messiah whispered. "This is the fourth or fifth offering with no prayer. They're extracting."

"Wait, it's not over. He'll spend maybe...uhm, five minutes on the word, leading to more offerings," Kenya said.

Just as Kenya said, the word was on Backbiting the Bishop and His Family.

"People are jealous of me and my wife because we're rich. We've been rich twice, and then became broke. Now I'm rich again and none of you've been able to do it not even once in your life. You gotta think, you gotta be creative. I've opened a school in North Carolina, and will be moving members down there, giving them jobs. Yes, we're moving forward in this ministry and if you can't see the vision, you'll miss the opportunity.

"Before we close, God's telling me someone's traveling this week. Raise your hand if you're traveling. C'mon, God's telling me someone is traveling. Don't leave without being blessed by me."

"Ah, Sistah Anderson, where are you going?"

"Uh uhm, my mother's sick. I'm leaving Friday for Alabama."

"Oh, well you know God can do anything but fail, don't you?"

She lifted her head up and dropped it, too overwhelmed to answer.

"Hmmm, the Lord's saying, you must write a check for five-hundred dollars, and not only will He guarantee a safe trip, but

He'll heal Mama. Praise the Lord, Saints!" He jumped up and down; his wife followed suit. Sister Anderson rushed to her seat, wrote the check, and put it in Garrison's hand. He said a quick prayer for her safe arrival, never mentioning her mother. "God's gonna work it out." Garrison used various hardship tactics before ending his offering escapade four-and-a-half hours later.

⚜

KENYA FROZE, HEARING THE KNOCK ON HER BEDROOM DOOR. "Kenya, I'm leaving. Thanks for everything. I really had a wonderful day," Messiah said.

"Leaving? Hold on. Wait a minute," Kenya said, rushing to slip her feet into her flip-flops. "Where are you going? You haven't eaten anything since this afternoon. Where are you gonna sleep?"

"Oh, I'll be fine. I know you're tired; so, I need to get out of your way. You're probably worrying about your neighbors and everything else."

"Psst, worrying about what?" Kenya lied. "At least have a snack. Aren't you hungry?"

"Well it—" He stopped when he saw the disappointment in her eyes. "Okay, let's have dessert together. After that I'll leave."

"Deal!" Kenya said, excitedly.

Kenya sliced the cantaloupe, putting half in each bowl. Messiah put away the dishes, opening up one cabinet after the next, until he found where everything belonged. "Why don't you just ask me, that would take less energy? Ya look crazy, opening every cabinet," Kenya teased.

"You-do-you, and I'll-do-me; after all, I'm making progress. The drainer's almost empty, isn't it?" He laughed.

"Sure is, five-hours later." Kenya laughed, plopping two scoops of ice cream atop each cantaloupe. They enjoyed their snack, talking and laughing. Kenya hated for the evening to end. It was the first time she'd felt alive since being with Tiffani and Trevor.

"Would you like something to drink?" Kenya asked.

"Uhm...water would be fine, thanks."

She retrieved two bottles of water. After thanking her, Messiah opened the bottle and took a long drink. "What's on your mind, Kenya?" He put the bottle down, giving her his full attention. "You look worried."

"I'm just thinking of the things I need to do, and decisions I need to make."

"Well they must be major, because your forehead has worry lines. Have you prayed?"

"Yeah, I was praying when you knocked on the door. I'm sorry for being a terrible host."

"My sister, you've been nothing but gracious." Messiah bowed his head to her humbly, placing his palms together. Kenya laughed and threw a napkin at him, "You are so crazy! Can I ask you a personal question?"

"Shoot. I've been through worse things than your questions."

"Where are you going? Is there a shelter I can drop you at? You know you're gonna have to label your stuff. Do you have plans? I know it's none of my business, but I can't help but worry." The silence in the room made Kenya uncomfortable; especially watching Messiah play with his hands. He raised his head to look at her; her forehead had creased deeper. Her cheekbones were clenched tight; her thoughts removed from the dessert she'd been eating. She was so preoccupied, she never heard Messiah speak. So he stopped mid-sentence until she released her train of thought.

"To answer your question, I don't know where I'm going. I

guess I need to check out some shelters until I find a job. I hope we can still spend time together, because I really enjoyed myself today."

"Messiah, I don't have much; but, I have a room with a bed in it. Would you like to stay here until you find a job? That way you can work, save your money, and put together your plan to save the world." She laughed to make the invitation less intense. "I've never done this before in my life; but, I feel in my heart that you won't harm me. I guess if you were gonna do something, you'd have done it before church, huh?" She laughed.

Messiah smiled. He knew her offer had emotionally wrecked her. "You're right about that, but I wouldn't make it a habit. If you prayed about this, I'll accept your offer. Any repairs and chores you have, I'll do. Thank you. I wasn't feeling the shelter, especially after I lost most of my stuff before."

❧ 18 ❧

SEEK YE FIRST HIS KINGDOM

K enya dropped her belongings on the floor and ran to the bathroom. She opened the bathroom door and peeped down the hall. Messiah's door was closed. Racing towards the stairs, she hoped she could reach her room before Messiah detected her mood.

Messiah was like a brother, but he stressed her, because he could find the spiritual approach to undo any situation. Worse, he could read her like his heart was attached to hers. *Tonight I'm not gonna talk about work. I'm grateful to be employed.*

"Colleen Burgus ruined your day, huh?" Messiah asked, holding his arms open to hug Kenya.

"Messiah please, not tonight," Kenya pleaded, falling into his arms. He took her belongings, grabbed her hand, and led her to the family room. "Sit." He patted his hand on the white leather loveseat. Kenya plopped down, laying her head on his shoulder.

"What did that Colleen do today?"

"I really don't wanna talk about this. That woman has been

our conversation every evening for a while. I'm tired of it, aren't you?"

"What I'm tired of is watching you handle it your way and not the way God intended," Messiah responded.

"*Me!* Are you crazy? How's this my fault? You weren't even there, and automatically I get blamed," she argued, standing up. "Geez, Messiah!"

Kenya and Messiah had been roommates for almost a year. They got along great until it came to their different approaches to handling problems. Kenya could not understand how Messiah would minimize every situation. He'd stop and pray. If he was having difficulty, he'd pray for guidance. If someone asked him to do something, he'd prayed before answering them.

She, on the other hand, would just go into a frenzy every time there was a problem, indulging in every emotion available. When Colleen Burgus waltzed into Kenya's department as Marketing Supervisor, Messiah warned Kenya that she was there for a reason. He told her he hoped that she'd learned enough from his teachings to handle her.

Obviously, I haven't learned a flippin thing, because I wake up miserable every morning, and come home drained every night. My only peace comes on the weekends and then I deal with Marian and Cassie, Kenya thought, no longer listening to Messiah.

"Come on, stop the dramatics. I didn't say it's your fault; I said you keep handling this woman the same way—"

"Go 'head, say it. I want you to say it! The same way I handle Marian. I'm not perfect like you. I don't know how to keep my emotions in check twenty-four seven. I don't know how to love someone while they kick me around, so just... say it. 'Kenya, you're an idiot!'"

"Watch your mouth, Kenya," Messiah said, firmly. "I didn't call you an idiot, nor do I think you are one, but hard-headed and overly-emotional come to mind."

Kenya stormed out the room, snatching her belongings off the top of the credenza by the door. Messiah stared at the back of her head as she exited, and then returned his attention to the news. *Lord, give her wisdom and patience where she's lacking. Open her heart to receive what I'm teaching her, and give her the strength to endure her lessons.*

Messiah fixed plates for both of them. He knocked twice and when Kenya did not answer, he opened the door. Kenya was sitting on the bed with her head slumped between her shoulders, playing with her hands. "I didn't say come in," she said, sarcastically.

"Girl, sit up. Your posture's terrible. Anyway, I prayed and you need to hear what I have to say." He plopped the tray on her lap, and left to get their drinks. When he returned, he sat in the chair across from her bed and ate his meal. Kenya took a sip of her juice, and held it away from her face, staring into the glass.

"I don't know what I'm doing wrong. I really don't understand how you think this is my fault." The tears rolled down her face. "I'm sorry for yelling at you."

"Kenya, I never said it was your fault. I said you're not handling it spiritually. Burgus isn't your battle. You take authority over the situation by taking anointing oil and going into that place, and pleading the blood of Jesus.

You speak every morning what you expect to see that day —*Peace!* You don't let *anyone* steal your joy. Do you play the Gospel CDs I made for you or read your scriptures before starting your day?"

"No," she whispered.

"What about praying for the strength to endure whatever

attack comes your way? Do you pray for Colleen, and her day to be touched by God?"

"Messiah, I pray every morning before I go to work."

"Do you pray for the things I mentioned?"

"Why should I pray for her? She ain't praying for me."

"Because she needs prayer. She's miserable."

"She's a Christian, going to church every Sunday. She's in the choir, and the dance ministry. We hear about it all the time."

"Do you know how many Christians go to church, Bible study, sing in the choir, even preach in the pulpit and don't have a clue of what Christianity is?"

"Christian is a title, *that's it*. That has nothing to do with what goes on inside of a person's mind or heart. Most people can only see the flaws of others; they have no conviction about their own wrongdoings, and they judge according to their standards. You have to pray for people caught up in the I-go-to-church-every-Sunday syndrome. Most people are caught up on titles. God's caught up on hearts.

If you see someone professing to be a Christian and they're not treating you accordingly, you need to pray for God to convict their hearts and pass judgment on the situation."

"Isn't that a selfish prayer, wishing harm on someone?" she asked, still sniffling.

"You're asking God to pass judgment so that if you're wrong, He'll make you see your errors and at the same time, deal with the other person's conscience accordingly.

"Colleen's problems are Colleen's. She's projecting them onto you. So it's your job to prevent her from making you the surrogate owner for her issues. Just like Marian, she makes her issues yours. She comes over unannounced, dropping the kids off without asking you. Then you continuously complain and stress. End it. Don't answer the door."

"That's rude!"

"Rude? How many times have you told her to call before coming, huh? What about the babysitting weeknights? Not opening the door when she brings the children is no more being rude than her showing up here. Sometimes it's you who has to change. Another thing, why are we still going to that dead church? There's no blessing in that. This man has people believing that they must pay him, so God can bless them.

"We've been on Matthew Chapter 11 for six months, and giving him money is his only message." Messiah laughed, getting up to go sit next to Kenya. "Why are we still there?" he asked again.

Kenya played with her hands before looking up at him. "*Fellowship*. God wants us to fellowship and since I'm tired of church-hopping, I go there." She lifted her eyes, shrugged her shoulders and fell back on her bed laughing. "That's horrible, isn't it?"

"Well if that's the case, we may as well form our own ministry here, because I know I can spiritually guide us better than Garrison Hughes."

"Boy, I could've told you that, but would we be fellowshipping?"

"We're fellowshipping right now. I've been thinking about starting a ministry of our own; maybe we could start it in your basement. What do you think?"

"I don't know... how would we do that? I hope you're not gonna recruit at different churches, especially not Hughes'."

"Girl, no. I was thinking about passing out flyers. You can invite people from work and your neighbors. Before you know it, people will start inviting others, and Warriors of Christ Ministry is birthed," Messiah said, taking a bow. Kenya clapped her hands, jumped off the bed and gave him a standing ovation.

"Sooooo, are you with me?" he asked, eagerly.

"I don't know, Messiah. I don't want them people from my job around me, and ugggh... Marian and Cassie. That's what you got for a congregation?" Kenya replied, flopping on her bed.

"*What?* Kenya, ministry isn't about us. That's why the world's still ruling, and people's lives are in such a mess. We have to reach out, take the good with the bad, the difficult with the easy and place all of it at the throne and let *God* do *Him*, change mud into gold. I know Marian and Cassie are difficult, but they're seeking God, and don't even know it. Why else would they go to church all the time?"

Messiah dragged the chair across the room and placed it in front of Kenya. He took both her hands in his, laying them on her lap. "Listen, a lot of people have this Christian life all miscon-strued. As Christians, we have responsibilities. Unfortunately, most think it's just about going to church, tithing, fellowshipping, and being baptized.

"It about here." He took her hand and laid it on the left side of her chest. "It's about Jesus giving the ultimate when he died for sin, giving all of us a second chance. Through our love and appre-ciation for Him, we're able to leave our wicked ways. Loving one another and the way we act, reflects what we feel about Him. When you love someone, don't you want to please them?"

Kenya whispered yes.

"That's what gets people to want to become a better person—a Christian. Their love for God makes them change from their wicked ways; that's not an easy task, either. Conviction will come from learning and beginning to play a major role in guiding people to do right." The tears rolled down Messiah's face. "The church is in you—it's in everyone—if you keep your door open right here." He tapped his chest.

Kenya reached for a tissue on her nightstand and gently wiped his face, and then hers.

"We need to educate ourselves with the Bible. Isn't that what Pastor Davenport pounded into your head? Embracing the Bible stimulates a desire for spiritual change. "Praying, thanking and praising God for everything He's done, and continues to do. We're supposed to seek God first. Our prayers must also be for others, even our enemies. And our needs shouldn't only be money and things we want. Growing spiritually in Him should be our main focus. He'll take care of the rest.

"We must teach others about our Father, His unconditional love, and His ultimate gift to mankind—Jesus Christ. We have to live a lifestyle that's acceptable to God, not us, respecting and loving each other, in spite of the challenges.

"It's not an easy job; most of the things require *sacrifice*. Helping to educate people like Marian, Cassie and Colleen requires patience. However, in doing so you make it possible for God to draw them to Christ. Then that's when the party begins, because it's that blood that seals us. It's that blood that heals, molds, and mends, making us brand new creatures." He threw his arms up in the air like he had just made a touchdown.

"That's what I want to do for people. Hopefully one day I can go to ministers like Hughes and Davenport, helping them understand the innocent lives they dismantled.

"For right now as God's children, our duty is to pray for those men because they too are lost. You pray and teach about Christ to people like the Marians, Cassies and Colleens of the world and just maybe something you say could change their lives. God changes us; not the church, not the preaching, not gospel songs, *God*. And He does it when He's ready and not a moment before."

Kenya hugged Messiah and kissed him on his cheek and thanked him for their lesson.

"Soooo, when do you want to do the flyers?" Kenya asked, sniffling. "After our little class; I wouldn't think of depriving anyone of your wisdom."

◌∕◌

KENYA PARKED ACROSS THE STREET FROM HER HOUSE, AND phoned Messiah to come and help unload the boxes. Ten boxes. She was proud of the designs she and Messiah had created.

"Wow, it looks great! Hopefully in three years we'll hold our first revival and when it's over, many ministers will rededicate. I'm so excited! Aren't you?"

"How're we gonna pay for this revival?" Kenya asked sarcastically.

"Big Daddy will handle that. Our responsibility right now is to gather His sheep. Maybe tonight we can get some people to hand out flyers." Messiah was excited about their first Bible study.

"Messiah, this is our first night and at this moment you only have one student, me." Kenya laughed, pointing at herself.

"Faith, Kenya, faith. We must trust God's ability to bring people. Did you tell Colleen, Marian, and Cassie?"

"I would have faith, but when it comes to people, uh...I'd just rather go on what I know, and uh ...uhmm no, I forgot to tell them."

"Why would you fabricate like that? You know you didn't forget. So for that you'll be assigned to be their mentor." Messiah laughed, briskly walking to the house with two boxes.

"You better run!" Kenya mumbled, pulling the box out of the trunk and stumbling backwards. She felt two arms reach around her, holding her and the box's weight. She looked up into the face of an extremely tall gorgeous-looking man.

"Oh, I'm sor—excus—; no, no," Kenya battled with her words. She looked him up and down, evaluating him. *Lord, all this muscle. Umm-umm-umm.* She closed her eyes and inhaled his cologne.

"Are you okay?" he asked, taking the box from her. Kenya cleared her throat. "Yes, thank you. Let me take that," she babbled.

"Where do you need it to go?" he asked, putting down the box to take off his jacket.

"Uhm, across the street, thank you."

"All these boxes are going over there?" he asked, scooping up another box before she could answer.

"Be careful," she said, watching him take long strides. She admired his long, caramel arms, filling out the sleeves of his tee-shirt. *Mmm, he's beautiful,* she thought, sitting down on the back of the truck.

"You know, I carried two boxes and you never told *me* to be careful or made sure *I* got across the street safely."

"Hush, Messiah. I was restin'. I've been working all day too and plus, you've got muscles and I wasn't—"

"Girl, slow down before you hurt yourself," Messiah teased, raising both his hands.

"What's up, man? I'm Adonyjah; I saw your wife struggling—"

"Thanks. I'm Messiah, this is Kenya." He shook his hand. "We aren't—"

"That's not my husband," Kenya snapped.

"No, her husband is upstairs resting; he's a police officer," Messiah said, then laughed.

"Messiah," Kenya whined, embarrassed that she never told him the truth.

"What? I was telling him I'm not your husband."

Kenya walked back to the truck to lock it, and when she returned across the street, she was amazed to find six boxes were in the house. Messiah and Adonyjah were standing at the top of the stairs in deep conversation with their arms folded.

"Hey, would anyone like a drink and a snack?" Kenya asked, smiling.

"Sure, thanks. I think I may have built up an appetite," Adonyjah replied. A wide-dimpled grin embraced his face.

❊

HERE I GO AGAIN, LETTING ANOTHER STRANGE MAN STROLL UP in here.

"He's ok," Messiah said, resting his hands on her shoulders.

"I'm not worried," Kenya responded.

"Come on, girl, be honest. The creases are running across your forehead. Oh, and by the way, that's your future husband; so, make that sandwich reveal your skills." Messiah laughed, walking out the kitchen.

Kenya felt a painless, unexplainable thud in her chest. She leaned on the counter, held her chest, took deep breaths, and then carried their meal into the dining room.

Messiah blessed the food, their lives and their union. They ate in silence for almost five minutes, and then Messiah asked Adonyjah about himself. Messiah observed the sadness in his voice when he talked about his family.

"Kenya, I was telling Adonyjah about the upcoming revival since he helped us."

"Yeah, Messiah believes he can make a difference, changing the direction of a lot of these churches."

"So what do you think?" Adonyjah asked.

"I think the patience he takes sitting through sermon after sermon on Sundays is commendable."

"Kenya, how can you say that when you're right there with me? Do you feel we're wasting our time?" Messiah asked, concerned with Kenya's vagueness about the question.

"You're not wasting my time because this is important to you, and I've nothing else to do."

"So in your travels, have y'all made assessments of any churches?" Adonyjah asked.

"Oh, I've assessed, I just don't wanna see Messiah disappointed when it's all said and done. People are people, especially church folks and preachers. Most of these preachers are about money and status. They're not about to listen to anyone; especially to someone they don't consider their equal. Don't get me wrong, I think Messiah knows more than most of them; I just don't know if they'll listen to him."

"You know, she does have a point. I stopped going to church years ago because... well, it doesn't really matter; but I understand what she's talking about," Adonyjah concluded, shifting his eyes from Messiah, to Kenya.

"Adonyjah, I realize you have to leave, but I want to share something with you two. Most leaders are concerned with money and status. They want the big church with the expensive markings and the large number of people, like people are cattle. They've left ministry responsibilities to a handful of ministers, which isn't enough to save all of God's sheep.

"Most of them have forgotten about their responsibilities and their ministerial description as men of God; they've tarnished what that blood stands for; it's now about monetary gain. Although, there are just a few who are not being responsible; it seems like a lot. In other words there are too many wolves in sheep's clothing.

"What's worse, no one calls them out, so people searching for God's help continue to wander aimlessly, never experiencing salvation. Something must be done."

"I don't know any scripture, so I don't know how I can help, but tell me what you need, maybe while I'm helping I can learn more," Adonyjah said.

"That's great, man! We'll expect God to bless our efforts, and have His way and expect nothing right now from the churches except that they attend the revival."

"Whoa whoa, Messiah." Adonyjah threw both his hands up in front of him, "Expect? I'm not expecting God to do anything; we're not trying to order Him around, are we? 'Cause I got enough problems with Him; I'm not bucking for more."

"I'm there with you. I'm trying to get on His good side," Kenya agreed.

Messiah buckled over laughing. "Expecting means having faith that God will grant your request. We have a lot of work ahead of us. When I'm finished with you two, you'll be true warriors!

"Count me in." Adonyjah laughed. "I got a two-for-one: food for the body, and food for the soul. I really wanna feel that confidence that we can make a difference, but I need to learn more stuff."

"The revival's in three years. Your confidence will come from learning and your faith that God's in control."

"So bro, what can I do to be a part of this mission?" Adonyjah asked.

"See, what I mean... *God*," Messiah whispered to Kenya.

"We have Bible study on Tuesday evenings right here. We devote ourselves on Wednesday evenings and Sundays to visiting churches, and putting our findings together for discussion.

"You're more than welcome to come, but it's a commitment. You'll have to sacrifice your Sundays, as well as Tuesday and Wednesday evenings. So, give thought to if this is something you think you'd be interested in. If not, then you're always welcome to join us for Bible study."

"Excuse me, I've gotta take this call," Adonyjah said, walking towards the front door. Kenya was washing dishes when Messiah walked into the kitchen. His smile extended across his face. "SSs-soo, Ms. Ye-of-Little-Faith, what do you think?"

"I don't know, Messiah, don't you think it's strange that he just jumped in and wanted to be involved?" Her face, etched with great concern, disturbed Messiah to see such mistrust.

"Kenya, we talked about faith. Don't you think this was God?" Messiah asked.

"Messiah, he's a stranger off the street who helped us. Plus, he drinks beer."

"And I was a homeless person. Yet amazingly, you opened your doors to me, a stranger, filthy, hungry, and without a toothbrush." They looked at each other intensely, and then laughed.

"Yeah, that was faith on both our parts, and now I thank God for you every day."

"What can I say?" Messiah asked, blowing on his fingers. "I is who I is. We've been a blessing to each other, believe me."

"If you feel he's alright, it's fine with me. Like I said, you're the head of this mission. I truly believe you hear from God, so I support what you do. You know, there's something I need to tell you, but don't get upset."

"Me, upset with you? Kenya there's nothing you can tell me that would upset me."

"I...uh... uhm, Messiah, I'm not married." Kenya dropped her head in embarrassment.

"Girl, I already knew that the first day. No man in his right mind's going to let some stranger move in his house. What bothers me is why it took you so long to tell me?"

"Well, in the beginning I was really afraid because I didn't know you; but then we clicked and I never thought about it again. It wasn't until today I realized I never told you. I trust you, Messiah, and—"

"Sorry, uh, that was my brother. I canceled my game; I'd like to attend your Bible class tonight before I commit. Can I bring my brothers?" Adonyjah asked.

"Sure, you're all welcome to come; the more the merrier. And please, don't think you have to join the mission to attend Bible study; that's a part of the mission, the mission isn't a part of Bible study."

❧

"Yeah, Marian, what's up?" Kenya asked.

"You, I haven't spoken to you since last week. What's going on? That man keeping you busy?"

"Marian, we've discussed this before; we're friends. I've told you this a million times," Kenya said, frustrated.

"I just don't understand why you can't see that man's fine. Can I have him?"

"That's up to Messiah; we're just roommates."

"Roommate! When did he become a roommate?" Marian shouted.

"I'm done. This conversation's becoming too much for me and I've got a lot to do. We're having Bible study tonight; Messiah's teaching. You wanna come?"

"Messiah's teaching? What the world does he know about the Bible?" Marian argued.

"It's at seven-thirty, you're welcome to come," Kenya said, patiently, "I gotta go."

"I'll be there," Marian finalized, then hung up the phone.

"You okay?" Messiah asked, concerned.

"Marian's supposedly joining us tonight," Kenya said, taking a long, deep breath. She started to leave the room, but turned back. "You know I keep trying to be friends with her, but it's not easy."

"Be patient with her, God will work it out. You're in her life for a reason, and it's God's reason, not yours," Messiah informed her.

"Trust me, Marian's not coming to enhance her spiritual growth. Actually, she's coming here for you, baaaabe!" Kenya laughed, pinching Messiah's cheek.

"She may be coming here for me, but she's going to get a good dose of Jesus-Juice." Messiah laughed.

❦ 19 ❦

IN THE IMAGE

Kenya and Messiah busied themselves setting up for their Bible study. Messiah was over-zealous; he lined the chairs, six across, in a row of five. He placed a notebook, Bible and pen in each seat.

"That's a lot of notebooks; you know something I don't?" Kenya asked.

"It's better to have more than not enough. You never know who'll show," Messiah said, confidently.

"Okay, Messiah, but we don't need to be wasting money. We should just get what we need and add on," Kenya advised.

"Yes ma'am. I'll take that into consideration next time; let's do faith tonight."

❦

"Messiah, get the door!" Kenya yelled. On the third

ring, Kenya opened the door. "What's up, Marian?" she half-greeted her, stepping to the side, oblivious to Marian's answer.

"Gurl, I was tryna get here first, for the 4-1-1 on everything," Marian replied, excitedly.

"Do you ever come out of nosy mode?" Kenya's anger was immediately interrupted by voices on the stairs. She stepped back in front of the door to see. "Hey, Adonyjah, glad you made it," Kenya said, transitioning from her scowl.

"Kenya, these are my brothers Aryngton, Alyxander and Adyson, my mother ZaBryna, Devon, his friend Trazie, and you know Zavian. Everybody, this is Kenya," Adonyjah said, proudly.

"C'mon in. This is Marian," Kenya said.

Marian spun on her heels, walking into the house. Kenya directed the group to the basement, and offered them water. When she returned upstairs, she confronted Marian about her rudeness to her guests.

"Gurl, they're gay. I met them at Zavian's before; none of them have girlfriends and they're always together." She was surprised that Kenya had not noticed.

"What does their sexual preference have to do with your nasty attitude? This is Messiah's and my home; we have the right to invite who we want without your judgment," Kenya chastised.

"Messiah's house? When did this become his house?"

"Marian, you need to respect whoever comes here; is that understood?" Kenya said, staying focused.

"Fine, if you wanna let trash up in your house, that's your business," Marian snarled, attempting to have the last word.

"Well if I was concerned about trash, I'da never invited you," Kenya snapped.

"What's going on here?" Messiah interrupted.

"She's got a problem with some people Adonyjah brought; she says they're gay. She called them trash."

"What's wrong, Marian?" Messiah asked, patiently.

"Two men together, Messiah? That's just nasty," she snapped.

"That's judging, Marian. You wouldn't want anyone judging you, would you? It's not our place to judge. These people are here for Bible study, and whatever they do away from here is no one's business. They're here to grow, to heal, and make constructive changes in their lives.

"That's what matters. The outcome of someone's life, not their lifestyle or situations. God will take care of all that in His time. Do you understand what I'm saying?"

"Yes," Marian answered, slumping her shoulders.

"Then let's go!" Messiah said, excitedly, putting his arms around both woman, hugging them.

જ₰ð

"GOOD EVENING, MY NAME'S MESSIAH JEHOVANAH," HE SMILED, "before we begin, I'd like to open with prayer. Anyone want to volunteer to lead us?" Messiah closed his eyes.

"Uh, Father God, we give you praise and honor for touching Messiah's heart to teach us," Devon began. He stuttered through most of his captivating prayer, and ended thanking God for their forgiveness, and protection. Devon looked around embarrassed. "I'm awful praying in front of strangers."

"Our heart is how God hears our prayers. Well, I guess we should start by sharing something about ourselves. Who wants to go first?" Messiah asked, looking around.

Heads turned from his direction whenever he looked at one of them. Finally, with no volunteers, he decided to arrange the chairs in a circle. Kenya sat to the right of Messiah, Adonyjah sat next to her, ZaBryna sat next to Adonyjah after he tapped the seat for her to sit. Aryngton, being protective, sat next to her. Devon, Trazie, Alyxander, Marian, Adyson, and Zavian closed the circle to the left side of Messiah.

The room was consumed with tension, so Messiah bowed his head and prayed for guidance.

"Wow, eleven of us, and not one decent story. How boring are we?" He laughed. "I'll go first. I'm Messiah, I'm thirty-three, I love ministering. I'm unemployed, but do odds jobs, including cleaning houses. I've been living in Maryland almost a year and I'm grateful you came to our first Bible Study tonight. So glad you want to embark on this spiritual journey with us."

He looked at Kenya asking her with pleading eyes to speak. He knew everyone would be more comfortable to follow her. After the second gentle elbow to her side, she spoke. "Hi, I'm Kenya Florenton, I work in marketing. I love to sing and dance. I'm happy Messiah started this ministry, and I'm surprised our first meeting is this successful. I hope everyone will continue to come, so we can grow together."

"I'm Adonyjah, I'm an engineer. I met Messiah and Kenya today; so glad I did. God and I don't have the best relationship, so maybe now I can find out why."

ZaBryna shook her head from side to side, her eyes fixed on her twirling hands.

"I'm Aryngton Clark, I have a twin, Aryn; I'm a regional manager. I'm glad to be here."

"I'm Devon Sherman, I'm a police officer. Donny, Alyx, Stud, Haze, Zave and me been having our own classes. We call ourselves, The Blind Leading the Blind. Messiah and Kenya, thank you for doing this. I heard about the revival; that's gonna be tight when we plan it."

Everyone waited patiently for Trazie until he looked at Alyxander. "I'm Alyxander Clark, I'm a stock clerk and I'm also in college. I want to thank Donny for bringing me here, and for being the backbone of our family. Messiah, I look forward to growing, and becoming part of your mission."

"I'm Marian Lloyd, I live across the street. I'm happy I came tonight and met all of you fine men. I hope to become a part of this family too." She laughed, and thought, *as soon as I make one of you fine-looking, caramel-skinned, loc-wearin', brothahs my husband.* Kenya elbowed Messiah throughout Marian's entire conversation.

"I'm Adyson Clark, they call me Haze, I also have a twin sis—"

"Two sets of twins, wow. I'm really gonna have to be careful when I get with one of you," Marian interrupted.

"Marian!' Kenya and Zavian shouted. "Go ahead, Adyson," Kenya said, cutting her eyes at Marian.

"There's really nothing more to tell. I was kinda dragged into this Jesus-Christ thing after I was released from prison, where I studied the Quran. I don't know why it matters, but I came tonight, because Donny was really impressed with you." Adyson plopped down, and dropped his head.

"I'm Zavian Bennings, I'm a lawyer. I'm excited about what you and Kenya have decided to do. Thank you for opening up your home."

"Adyson, we thank God for your attendance tonight," Messiah said, rubbing his chest, feeling Adyson's anguish. "Since tonight's our first class, maybe we'll keep it light; so the first thing we'll focus on is ourselves. Once you know who you are in Christ, you'll set standards for yourselves, and limitations for others." ZaBryna lifted her head.

Messiah spent the evening teaching them they were children of God, regardless of what flaws they had, crimes they committed, or what anyone had told them. "You must understand that God's your father. He won't neglect, or dismiss you when you do something wrong. He'll comfort you at any time, through any situation. Even when you share your deepest, darkest secrets with Him, He's there for you." He swung his pointed finger to each of them.

"He's there in the morning, before the sun rises; the midday when everyone's hustling to and fro in the evening; when you're exhausted, and throughout the night as you sleep. He'll never forsake you.

"Now, He might sit quiet sometimes to see if you trust Him, but He's there." Everyone was captivated. Most sat, slightly bent over, with their elbows on their knees as though they would miss something if they sat back. Periodically, someone would raise their hand, and ask a question; once it was answered, they resumed their position.

"God is your Father, friend, companion, confidante, doctor and lawyer. He's anything you need him to be, when you need Him. And what makes us so great, is we're all made in God's image."

"This book is God's love story to us." He held up his Bible. "Genesis Chapter one, Verse twenty-seven says, *"So God created man in his own image, in the image of God created he him; male and female created he them."* Messiah looked at them with the biggest smile on his face. "What does that mean?" he asked, excitedly.

"We're *fantastic people*." Zavian laughed.

"Exactly! How many of us are *not* made in God's image?"

No one raised their hands, but the body language from ZaBryna, Adonyjah, Adyson, Kenya, Alyxander and Aryngton revealed their answer. Some dropped their heads, some shoulders slumped, and some became fidgety; Adyson's body did everything.

Thank you, Lord. We have a lot of building up to do in here. "Where's the word e-x-c-e-p-t in this verse?" Messiah asked. Everyone busied themselves looking, "Except isn't even there," Adyson snarled.

"*Correct!*" Messiah said, slapping his hand on the book. "There are no exclusions; so all of us are made in God's image."

"Ouuuu!" ZaBryna groaned, grabbing her chest.

"You okay?" Aryngton asked. She nodded her head yes, as tears raced down her face. She grabbed Adonyjah's and Aryngton's hands, trying to compose herself. Aryngton focused on her fingers, bending them, while Adonyjah rocked nervously from side to side.

Kenya stared at the side of Messiah's face, slowly raising her head up and down, astonished.

Devon's head bounced up and down. When he made eye contact with Messiah, he gave him the thumbs up. *Yeah, this is it! Thank you, Lord; goodbye, Blind Leading the Blind!*

Trazie sat with the same scowl on his face he had when he arrived. Alyxander was focused on picking invisible lint off his pants.

Marian was rubbing Adyson's back while he rocked back and forth uncontrollably; his tears flowed accordingly. And Zavian's hands were lifted in praise.

Messiah looked around, smiling, "This is good. Before we close in prayer, I want you all to remember one important thing: "God loves all of us. He loves you, you..." Messiah pointed to each of them, calling them by name, then said, "...and me!"

ABOUT THE AUTHOR

Marjaye Free was born to write. A dynamic author with a powerful message, Free has always had a passion for helping others. *Test Run: In His Image* is Free's first fictional voyage into her first love—writing. When not crafting inspired literature, Marjaye Free operates and owns a family daycare full of learning, laughter, and much-needed naptimes.

Free is the mother of three and a native of Brooklyn, NY. Currently living in Bowie, MD, Free is a model of how to be a fighter and survivor. No matter what life has thrown her way, Marjaye Free has never given up on her dream. This book is her message to readers to keep going.

While *Test Run: In His Image* is her first fiction series, it's far from her last. According to the author, she has many more books inside. Free hopes to release Book 2 in this series very soon. If you loved this story, just wait until you see what happens next!